Bronwyn curled up, lying on her side and hugging her knees to her, even though it stretched her tender muscles to do so. She closed her eyes and tried not to think about how bad she felt.

This must be what Mommy feels. Only she's never gonna get to go home.

The thought made her sad. It was something she'd known for a long time, but tried not to think about. Being in the hospital for one day was terrible; what must it be like to stay for years?

Her father had said her mother wasn't aware of anything, so her mother wasn't sad at what had happened to her; but Bronwyn didn't see how that could be. Even asleep last night, she'd known she wasn't in her own bed at night.

Wasn't a coma the same as being asleep?

"Mommy," she cried, sobbing. "Mommy, please come and take me home."

In another room, in another wing, her mother's eyes popped open. . . .

THRILLERS BY WILLIAM W. JOHNSTONE

THE DEVIL'S CAT   (2091, $3.95)

The town was alive with all kinds of cats. Black, white, fat, scrawny. They lived in the streets, in backyards, in the swamps of Becancour. Sam, Nydia, and Little Sam had never seen so many cats. The cats' eyes were glowing slits as they watched the newcomers. The town was ripe with evil. It seemed to waft in from the swamps with the hot, fetid breeze and breed in the minds of Becancour's citizens. Soon Sam, Nydia, and Little Sam would battle the forces of darkness. Standing alone against the ultimate predator — The Devil's Cat.

THE DEVIL'S HEART   (2110, $3.95)

Now it was summer again in Whitfield. The town was peaceful, quiet, and unprepared for the atrocities to come. Eternal life, everlasting youth, an orgy that would span time — that was what the Lord of Darkness was promising the coven members in return for their pledge of love. The few who had fought against his hideous powers before, believed it could never happen again. Then the hot wind began to blow — as black as evil as The Devil's Heart.

THE DEVIL'S TOUCH   (2111, $3.95)

Once the carnage begins, there's no time for anything but terror. Hollow-eyed, hungry corpses rise from unearthly tombs to gorge themselves on living flesh and spawn a new generation of restless Undead. The demons of Hell cavort with Satan's unholy disciples in blood-soaked rituals and fevered orgies. The Balons have faced the red, glowing eyes of the Master before, and they know what must be done. But there can be no salvation for those marked by The Devil's Touch.

Available wherever paperbacks are sold, or order direct from the Publisher. Send cover price plus 50¢ per copy for mailing and handling to Zebra Books, Dept. 2917, 475 Park Avenue South, New York, N.Y. 10016. Residents of New York, New Jersey and Pennsylvania must include sales tax. DO NOT SEND CASH.

LULLABYE

PATRICIA WALLACE

ZEBRA BOOKS
KENSINGTON PUBLISHING CORP.

ZEBRA BOOKS

are published by

Kensington Publishing Corp.
475 Park Avenue South
New York, NY 10016

First printing: March, 1990

Printed in the United States of America

For Andy
and
For Leslie
who believed

Tuesday's child is full of grace. . . .

1982

Prologue

Wyatt English had been a doctor long enough to know that bad things happened even on the most beautiful of spring days, but until today the bad things had always happened to someone else.

The concept of being the one addressed in the somber, grave tones reserved for the next of kin of a critically ill patient was so foreign to him that he had difficulty listening to what was being said. That and the sunlight which flooded the hallway outside of Radiology left him temporarily mute.

"We'll do what we can," the neurosurgeon said, "but the brain scan indicates a massive hemorrhage into the posterior fossa. A blown aneurysm, no doubt. A congenital flaw would be my guess, since she has no prior history of hypertension. At any rate, a bleed like this . . . you understand that it may not be survivable, no matter what we do."

The anesthesiologist inclined her head in agreement. "As for the baby, the outlook is better. The fetal heart tones are good; the baby hasn't been compromised as of yet. Your wife's obstetrician is on

11

his way in. As soon as he gets here we'll go straight into surgery and . . . take the baby."

They seemed to expect a response from him, but he didn't trust himself to speak. He nodded instead, his mind racing at the impossibility of it all. This morning when he'd left the house, Deborah had been fine, eight months pregnant and vibrantly alive.

"After the baby is delivered, we'll admit—Deborah, is it?—to ICU and see if we can relieve the pressure on the brain." The neurosurgeon paused, frowning. "That is, if she makes it through the C-section."

Instinctively Wyatt knew that neither of them believed she would.

The anethesiologist, an intense young woman whom he'd never had occasion to speak to until today, reached out and touched his arm. "Does she have family? You might want to call them. Just in case."

That jolted him out of his silence. "I'm her family," he said. "I'm all she has."

And she's all I have that matters.

The neurosurgeon's eyes shifted, looking beyond him, down the hallway. He turned as Deborah's obstetrician—she'd laughingly referred to him as Doc Holiday because he was always jetting off on one exotic vacation after another—walked up.

Wyatt saw the look that passed between the three of them and felt his own expression change in response, as though the muscles of his face knew something his mind had yet to truly comprehend.

"Wyatt," the obstetrician said, "I'm so sorry."

Without warning, his eyes filled and he closed them momentarily, fighting for control, and regaining it.

For a moment no one spoke.

And then, knowing as he spoke that he shouldn't, knowing that the words would only serve to negate

12

his professional standing and reduce him in their eyes to just one more desperate husband, he said quietly, "Don't let her die."

He signed the forms admitting Deborah Ann English into the hospital, a surgical consent for the cesarean, and an assignment of insurance benefits. For the first time since he'd finished medical school, he signed without including the M.D. after his name.

Assured by the charge nurse that someone would notify him when they brought Deborah out of O.R., he sought refuge in the hospital's chapel.

The stained-glass windows gentled the bright California sun, casting a warm multihued glow in the small room. Wyatt walked to the front and sat, his eyes drawn to the plain white cross on the wall behind the pulpit.

Alone, silent, he waited.

Was there comfort to be found in this place? Even in his anguish, he doubted.

Medicine had taught him that disease was no respecter of good, no punisher of evil. In his experience, even the most fervent of prayers could not reverse sepsis or restore lungs made brittle from a lack of surfactant.

Whispered pleas to God for relief from pain were answered by the administration of a narcotic, and not by heavenly intervention.

His faith was in physiology, biology, biochemistry. He trusted in—and relied on—the technology.

He could see the electric tracings of the heart on a cardiac monitor screen. He could hear the sound of blood pulsing through an artery. He could feel the contour of a mass hidden within the recesses of the human body. And he could smell the sweet scent of decay that so often preceded death.

These things were real, tangible. They existed. So much of what he dealt with as a physician was black or white. Even the shades of gray, the nuances, were quantifiable to a degree.

But medicine, for all the faith he placed in it, had not prepared him for this.

More than anything, he wanted to call time out. He wanted it all to stop, for the seconds to quit ticking by, for time to be suspended while he went back to medical school and through his residency again, so he could learn what he'd need to know to save Deborah's life.

If he had it to do over—if only—he would save her with his own hands.

Tradition held that doctors shouldn't treat members of their own families, but if he had it within his power to save her, tradition be damned.

Deborah was the focus of his life, the nucleus around which he revolved. From the day they'd met, there had been no one else for him

She *had* to pull through this. Had to. If praying would help, then by God, he'd pray.

At two-thirty a nurse came and told him that he was the father of a baby girl.

Deborah had wanted a girl. And after months of indecision, she'd finally chosen a name.

But he couldn't think about that now. "How is my wife?" he asked.

"I can't say, Dr. English; I work in the nursery. The baby is fine, though. She's a tiny one—five pounds, ten ounces; and eighteen inches long."

He stared at her, trying to fathom whether she was deliberately avoiding telling him what he was afraid to hear.

"The baby's Apgar was a solid ten," the nurse

14

continued, apparently oblivious to the intensity of his gaze. "You can come up and see her if you'd like."

"I . . . not now. Later." Wyatt fought against his own impatience. "You haven't heard anything about my wife's condition?"

"No, I'm sorry."

He wanted to question her further, but realized that it would be to no avail. Even if she knew something, she wouldn't say; it was the doctor's province to deliver news, good or bad.

In an odd way, he was relieved. He wasn't ready, yet, to give up hope.

Was anyone ever ready?

"She's a darling little baby." The nurse smiled, but her eyes were sad. "I *am* sorry, Dr. English," she said, and was gone.

The afternoon passed.

At ten to five, the door to the chapel opened and Wyatt looked up.

"Ah," the neurosurgeon said. "Here you are."

He stood, filled with dread. Their eyes met and held, and that alone told him that Deborah was, at least, still alive. "How is she?"

"Holding her own. She's in Intensive Care; they're doing an EEG."

Wyatt didn't want to think of what that could mean, but there was no avoiding it. An EEG would determine whether her brain was functioning. Which meant they suspected it wasn't. "And?"

"*And* we'll see." His tone was grim. "It's too soon to say."

Wyatt detected the subtle chastisement. He was asking questions they both knew could not be answered. He looked away, but not before noticing a fine spray of dried blood on the surgeon's scrub suit.

"You can go up to ICU and see her," the neurosurgeon said, and ran a hand through his short-cropped gray hair. "But I think you should . . ." His voice trailed off.

"Should what?" Wyatt prompted.

The neurosurgeon shook his head. "Nothing. Never mind. Go up and see your wife. This has been one hell of a long day."

The eight beds in ICU were arranged in a semicircle, extending from the hub of the nursing station. He checked at the desk with the unit secretary who informed him that Deborah was in seven.

A pale green curtain had been drawn around the bed for privacy, and Wyatt hesitated for a moment before pulling it back.

His breath caught in his throat at the sight of her.

Earlier that afternoon, when they'd called him out of the Utilization Committee meeting and informed him that his wife had been brought to Emergency, he'd thought only that she must have gone into labor a month ahead of time.

No one had had time to tell him any different; when he'd made it down to E.R., the place was pure bedlam.

An ambulance had arrived with several bloodied victims of an auto accident, two of them children, both of whom were screaming at the top of their lungs.

A man who looked to be in his mid fifties held center stage in the Code Room, suffering from an apparent heart attack and evidently souring fast.

And a young Hispanic man had been brought in

16

from a local foundry where he'd somehow managed to pour molten lead into his calf-high boot. The stench of burned flesh hung heavy in the air.

Somewhere amid all of the turmoil was Deborah, probably awaiting transfer up to the Obstetrical Floor. He imagined her telling the nurse not to bother with her, to take care of the others instead—

Then he'd caught a glimpse of her as they'd rushed her to Radiology. Ashen, her features slack, her mouth slightly agape, and with the twin lines of the nasal oxygen cannula dissecting her face, she'd looked frighteningly unfamiliar to him.

For a few seconds he'd thought that it was a mistake, that it wasn't Deborah at all. But he'd seen the wedding ring he'd had made for her on her left third finger—an amethyst and five small diamonds in an antique gold setting—and all doubt had vanished.

Now, standing at her bedside, he had to convince himself anew that this was his beloved Deborah.

She looked desperately ill, as ill as anyone could look and still survive.

Her complexion was paler yet, almost bloodless, and even though she was now receiving oxygen via the MA-1 respirator, she was cyanotic, her lips tinged blue.

The fine bones of her face seemed to have coarsened, her cheekbones starkly prominent, giving her almost a skeletal appearance.

They had tucked her long blond hair beneath a paper surgical cap, but wisps of it had escaped, adhering to her skin which was damp with perspiration.

Even mechanically assisted, her breathing was erratic, the rise and fall of her chest barely perceptible.

Wyatt touched his fingers to her wrist, momentarily reassured by the flutter of her pulse.

"Deborah," he whispered, "don't leave me."

The neurosurgeon came by near midnight to tell him that the results of the EEG they'd done showed limited and wildly sporadic brain activity.

"She isn't brain dead," the neurosurgeon said, "but her brain waves are clearly dysfunctional. There's a fire storm of electrical activity going on in her brain right now. How long it'll continue, or what'll happen when it stops, I can't predict. But the prognosis is unchanged. I don't believe she'll make it through the night."

Wyatt thought he had become numb by now, but he was wrong.

"It might be hours, or at the most a few days." The neurosurgeon rested a hand on Wyatt's shoulder. "At least she's not in pain. And the baby is fine. Be thankful for that."

Someone finally thought to bring him a chair, and he sat at her bedside, stroking her hand, and fearing that each breath she took would be her last.

Behind him the curtain parted, and an ICU nurse approached the bed, a capped syringe in hand. She nodded a greeting but didn't speak.

The nurse removed the plastic sheath from the needle which she inserted into the three-way stopcock, infusing the milky fluid into the intravenous line.

He wondered why they would give her medication if they expected her to slip away, but before he could ask, the nurse had disappeared.

Briefly he considered going to the nursing station to read the chart, but he didn't want to leave Deborah. He would never forgive himself if the moment came and he wasn't with her.

Hours or days, however long she had left, he would stay with her.

But when morning came, she was hanging on, clinging tenuously to life.

No one expected her to make it through Wednesday, but she did. A second EEG mirrored the first, and a neurologist called in for a consultation suggested that the frenzied tracings of the brain's activity were reminiscent of an electrical short circuit.

"I've never seen anything quite like it," he added sotto voce as they left the bedside. "It is spectacular, though, isn't it? The amount of energy involved . . ."

On Thursday, Wyatt fell asleep in the chair, and woke in a cold sweat, having hallucinated that he had heard the alarm on the cardiac monitor and scared beyond measure that the end was imminent.

But Deborah, deep in a coma, held on. And as the day passed, her vital signs began to stabilize. By late afternoon there were indications that she was fighting the respirator, as though trying to breathe.

The decision was made to take her off the MA-1.

To the astonishment of her doctors, and after a brief episode of apnea, during which Wyatt's own heart rate raced, she resumed breathing. Shallow breaths, somewhat labored, but breathing all the same.

Arterial blood gases were drawn to determine whether the oxygen saturation level was adequate; remarkably, it was.

"This doesn't mean she'll recover," the neurologist cautioned. "Only that the brain stem is functional. I don't have to tell you that breathing is an instinctual and not a purposeful act."

"Yes, I know."

"She is totally unresponsive."

"Like the Quinlan case," the neurosurgeon added. "There's no cognitive function, nor hope of any. She's in a chronic persistent vegetative state."

Wyatt listened to them and offered no argument. He was advised that at some point Deborah would have to be transferred to an extended-care facility equipped to handle long-term comatose patients.

"A young woman such as she is might last for years before her system breaks down."

No one came right out and said it, but he understood that they needed the ICU bed for someone who had a chance at resuming a normal life.

Deborah's life—and his—had irreparably changed.

On Saturday, he went to the nursery and saw their child for the first time.

She was tiny, with dark eyes and the promise of her mother's blond hair. Her fingers closed around his thumb with a strength that surprised him.

As Deborah had wished, he named her Bronwyn Grace English.

A day later, he took his daughter home.

1990

One

Thursday, June 14th

When the lunch bell sounded, Bronwyn English put her math book on her desk and hurried to the back of the classroom to get her lunch pail.

Miss Peters stood by the door, assuring order as they left for the cafeteria.

"Young ladies and gentlemen don't run in the halls," Miss Peters said, although nobody was running, at least not while she could see them.

Bronwyn walked like a little lady until she reached the turn in the corridor and then ran as fast as she could after the others, giggling as she jostled and was jostled by her classmates.

The best tables were by the windows which faced out on the school's central courtyard. When they reached the double doors leading into the cafeteria, Bronwyn ducked under the arm of the fifth grader in front of her, took two quick steps, and then slid the rest of the way across the polished wood floor.

Tennis shoes were great for running, but nothing beats the smooth soles of brand new patent leather dress shoes at sliding.

Her reward was the coveted end seat at the table nearest the exit.

For a moment, she savored her victory, looking out the tinted windows, all else forgotten. The voices around her faded until she heard nothing but the imagined sigh of wind as it rustled through the trees.

Shaded by huge elms and always breezy, the courtyard was, to her, a very special place. Bayview Elementary sat on a bluff overlooking the Pacific Ocean, and the view filled her with a sense of wonder.

Blue-green waves crested in white peaks and then battered themselves against the rocks. There wasn't a beach to speak of, but there were tide pools and, she suspected, even caves.

All of it was off limits. A chain-link fence bordered the school grounds, caging them in. Protecting them, the teachers said, from the unstable edge of the cliffs which had been known to give way.

Hardly a day went by that Bronwyn didn't find herself at the fence, her fingers curled around the rusting metal links, her face pressed against it. Sometimes the bigger waves would crash and a fine spray would drift up, cooling her with its salty tang.

Freedom was on the other side of the fence, and this was the summer she would taste it. School was out tomorrow and this summer—

"Are you gonna eat or just sit there?" The voice intruded on her thoughts.

Bronwyn blinked and looked across the table where Kenny Dodd grinned at her, gap-toothed.

"I'm eating." She opened her lunch pail.

"What've you got?"

Kenny was eight, as she was, and not fat exactly, but big for his age, nearly the size of the haughty sixth-grade kids. Food never went to waste when Kenny was around; he even ate the cream cheese and lox and bagels that everyone else wrinkled their noses at.

Bronwyn frowned at her lunch. The housekeeper, Mrs. Henderson, had a thing about nutrition, and there were neat Baggies full of carrot and celery strips, plus a cored apple and what was probably chicken salad on whole wheat bread. The thermos was filled with milk. Plain white milk, not even chocolate.

"I've changed my mind. I think I'll just sit here," she said, and pushed the pail toward Kenny. At least she'd had a good breakfast.

He rummaged through it. "What, no Twinkies?"

"Have I ever had Twinkies?"

"Jeez. For a doctor's daughter, you sure don't eat rich."

"We're not rich," she said.

Kenny wedged carrot sticks in the spaces between his front teeth, imitating Dracula, she supposed. As big as he was, Kenny still acted like a kid.

"Sure," he lisped around the carrot sticks. "You got that monster house and a maid—"

"A housekeeper," Bronwyn corrected. Mrs. Henderson would hate being called a maid.

"And your dad practically owns the hospital. If I had that much money, I'd buy a McDonald's and pig out on burgers every day."

Bronwyn said nothing. She'd never eaten at McDonald's.

"No wonder you're so skinny," he said. "Don't you ever eat anything that's not good for you?"

She was saved from answering when Jason Cochran came up to the table, carrying a tray. "Move over," he ordered, and Kenny complied.

Jason was only a grade ahead of them, but somehow he had gotten in with the big kids, and no one dared question his right to sit where he wanted. It was probably, she thought, because one of his older brothers was the star quarterback on the high-school football team.

Rumor had it that Jason liked her, and he smiled at her now.

Bronwyn lowered her eyes. She'd heard a teacher say that all of the Cochran boys were precocious. She wasn't sure what that meant, but it sounded vaguely dangerous, as if someone ought to build a fence around *them*.

"Jeez," Kenny said. "You're actually gonna eat that meat loaf?"

"No, I'm gonna let you eat it. If you don't die, then I'll feed it to my dog."

Bronwyn hid a smile. It wasn't a nice thing to say, but Kenny was always going on about how bad the school's food was, even as he was wolfing it down.

Kenny, agreeable as always, reached over and helped himself to a bite of meat loaf, eating with his fingers and then licking them clean. "Not bad. You know, it kinda looks like dog food, doesn't it?"

She glanced at Jason and caught him looking at her. Precocious, she reminded herself, feeling the heat of a blush coloring her cheeks.

"So what are you doing this summer?" Jason asked Kenny, although somehow she knew the question was really directed at her.

Kenny snorted. "My folks are taking me and my sister to Yosemite to feed us to the bears."

"Huh. Poor bears." Jason twirled the handle of his fork between his thumb and forefinger. "What about you, Bronwyn? What are you doing?"

She lifted her shoulders in a shrug. "Just going to my dance class. And to the beach," she said, more

26

deterined than sure.

"You're not going away?"

"No. My dad's too busy to take a vacation." She reached across the table and took a few corn chips from the bag that Kenny had open. They crunched satisfactorily and she took a couple more.

"I'm staying, too."

"Oh."

Nearly everyone in town left during the summer; by the Fourth of July, the beaches and restaurants and stores would be swarming with tourists, and the locals—at least those who didn't make money off the summer people—went away, or, as her father said, "headed for the hills."

"Maybe I'll see you at the beach," Jason said.

"Maybe." Bronwyn didn't want to admit that she might not get to go.

In fact, Mrs. Henderson had always refused to take her, saying that the damp air made her arthritis act up. But for the first time since she'd come to work for them, when Bronwyn was four years old, the housekeeper was taking a vacation of her own, two full months' worth, and flying off to visit a sister in Iowa.

She was keeping her fingers crossed that whoever her father hired to take over for Mrs. Henderson wouldn't share the housekeeper's affliction.

"Which beach do you usually go to?" Jason asked.

Bronwyn shrugged again, embarrassed by his persistence. "I don't know. By the lighthouse?"

"Maybe," Kenny said with a smirk, "you can see each other at dance class."

Jason ignored him. "I go there all the time."

"Oh." She didn't know what else to say, so she nodded, closed her lunch pail, and got up to leave.

27

She could feel him watching her as she walked away.

There were fluffy white clouds in the sky, and Bronwyn shaded her eyes to look up at them as she headed toward the fence. Not the kind of clouds that rained, she decided, but pretty just the same.

California was in the middle of a drought, although it was worse in the southern part of the state. She'd been born in Los Angeles, but they'd moved to Hansen's Point when she was still a baby because the town had the kind of hospital her mother needed.

Thinking of that reminded her that today was a visiting day. Mrs. Henderson would pick her up after school and take her to the hospital where she would sit with her mother for fifteen or twenty minutes.

It wasn't bad, really. Sometimes she did her homework, or practiced dance steps, but mostly she just sat. Sometimes she talked to her mother, even though she knew her mother couldn't hear her.

When she was younger she used to imagine that she saw her mother's eyelids flutter, and she would wait, breathless with excitement, for her to wake up. Then when she was five her father sat her down and gently explained to her about comas.

What he'd told her had made her cry.

Now, staring through the fence at the swell of the sea, she wondered how it felt to be in a coma, to live without ever waking.

Her father said that there was no pain, but Bronwyn wondered. She'd seen bruises on her mother's arms where they took blood, and more than once she'd overheard the nurses talking about bedsores or an abscess.

She'd gone into her father's library and found a

book with pictures. He had lots of books, and there were all kinds of colored pictures. Looking at them left her feeling sick.

It *had* to hurt, to have an open wound.

After seeing the pictures, the first thing she did when she entered her mother's room was pull the sheet up, so that if there were bruises she wouldn't know.

The problem was, she still knew there were bruises. And worse.

She'd grown up hearing words like strictures, and atrophy, and brittle bones. Other words grew familiar to her as well: catheters, blood gases, serum potassium levels, cerebral pressure, and ischemia.

The first time she'd heard of CAT scans, she'd been intrigued, even amused. Her father told her that the scans didn't hurt, but her mother often had a bad day after having one.

The scariest word of all was prognosis. It meant, her father said, the prospect of recovery.

Her mother hadn't any.

The outcome was certain. Only the when of it was in doubt.

Bronwyn tightened her grip on the fence. The wind wrapped her skirt around her legs and blew her hair across her face. A cloud passed the sun and cast its shadow on her. She shivered.

The bell sounded behind her, calling her back to class. By this time tomorrow, school would be out for the year.

Summer beckoned. . . .

Two

"This is going to sting," Wyatt English said, and carefully inserted the needle beneath the skin above the spine.

The patient, a nineteen-year-old Army private from Fort Ord, was too ill to protest. He lay motionless on his side, knees drawn up tight, his head tucked toward his body, his spine in hyper-flexion. As still as he was, the nurse held him firmly, to keep him from moving.

The young soldier had come into the hospital complaining of a severe headache and a stiff neck. He was running a temperature of 101.8° which aspirin hadn't helped. According to the friend who'd accompanied him, he'd had a sore throat earlier in the week which had gone untreated.

He had vomited twice since being admitted into E.R., and appeared to be increasingly drowsy, nearly to the point of stupor.

The symptoms were classic for acute bacterial meningitis, which flourished in the close confines of Army barracks. A year before two recruits had died from a particularly virulent outbreak of meningo-coccus meningitis, with half a dozen others requiring

31

hospitalization before the disease ran its course.

A lumbar puncture was necessary to confirm the diagnosis; laboratory examination of the cerebrospinal fluid would determine the organism at hand.

Wyatt injected Xylocaine subcutaneously to anesthetize the area, gave it a minute to take effect, then pushed the needle in deeper, almost to the bone. When he had emptied the syringe he withdrew it, and tossed it onto the procedure tray.

He picked up the larger lumbar puncture needle with one hand, using the other to palpate the depression between the third and fourth vertebrae. By now the anesthetic would have done its job; the patient would feel pressure as he did the tap, but no pain.

"Keep him still," he said to the nurse. Pain or not, sometimes the patient tried to move.

Wyatt stuck the needle through the skin, angling it slightly upward and keeping it perpendicular to the spine. He approached the vertebrae at midline, and guided the needle to the dura. A momentary resistance as he punctured the dura, and then the needle was in the spinal canal. He withdrew the stylet from the needle.

Drops of cerebrospinal fluid appeared at the needle bevel. Normally clear and colorless, this sample was cloudy, indicating an elevated concentration of bacterial cells, and the color of straw, which was indicative of the presence of protein.

Wyatt used the manometer to measure the CSF pressure, which was, as suspected, above the high-normal range of two hundred millimeters.

He collected the specimens in several small plastic vials which he placed upright in the rack provided and then nodded at the lab technician who'd been standing by.

"Be sure to do a gram stain," he called after the tech

as she hurried out of the examining room. To the patient he said, "Almost done."

A second check with the manometer showed a slight decrease in CSF pressure. He deftly removed the needle, then covered the puncture site with a sterile dressing, taping it in place.

"That's it," he said, and stepped back.

"Very nice." The nurse released her hold. "Fastest tap in the West."

Wyatt stripped off the latex gloves and came around the side of the gurney. The patient's eyes were closed. "How are you doing?" he asked. "Hanging in there?"

The young man gave a barely perceptible nod, but didn't answer.

Wyatt rested his hand on the soldier's shoulder. "All right, let's get him admitted to isolation on the medical floor. We'll start him on Penicillin G, two hundred thousand units per kilogram q four hours. He's dehydrated, so hang a thousand cc's of five percent dextrose, and make sure the lab runs electrolytes on his blood."

"Right away, Dr. English."

Wyatt stopped by the nursing station to write up the admitting orders for his patient, and noticed that it was a few minutes past one o'clock.

"Damn."

The clerk looked up from her filing. "Is something wrong?"

"I have an appointment at one, I'm late, and I'm going to be later." He sat down, grabbed a blue physician's order sheet and a pen, and began to fill out the form, writing as fast as he could.

"Doctors are always late. Patients expect it. That's why they're called patients."

He shook his head. "This isn't a patient. I'm interviewing a summer replacement for my housekeeper. Who is leaving tomorrow."

The clerk laughed. "Nothing like waiting 'til the last minute, is there?"

"I didn't plan to."

"No? I think narrowly averting a crisis is in every doctor's blood."

"I wouldn't say that."

She waved a sheaf of lab test results at him. "Admit it. You're addicted to that adrenaline rush you get when all hell breaks loose."

Wyatt laughed in spite of himself. "It's an interesting theory, but I don't think it applies to me."

"You're way too modest—" The phone rang and she reached for it. "Saved by the bell. Emergency," she said into the receiver.

He signed the order sheet, clipped it to the E.R. chart, and placed it on top of the stack. Another glance at the clock propelled him out of the chair.

His office was located in a small medical building across the street from the hospital, and he cut across the parking lot, heading in that direction.

"Wyatt," a voice called from behind.

He turned, walking backward as he scanned the lot and hoping that it would be someone he could wave to and be on his way.

It wasn't.

Percy Smitson barreled toward him, the human equivalent of a Sherman tank. Not in appearance—he stood a scant five feet and was a pale-complected redhead—but definitely in attitude.

"Glad I caught you," he said, huffing a little as he approached.

"Percy."

"Have a minute? Good."

"Actually," Wyatt tapped at the face of his watch, "I'm a little pressed for time."

"Nice watch," Smitson said. "Listen, I've gone over those figures we were talking about—for a trauma unit?—and I have to tell you, looking at the bottom line, it's a 'no go.'"

Wyatt felt a flash of annoyance. "We need to upgrade our emergency facilities, Percy. People's lives are at stake here."

"Hey, I'm all for saving lives, but this is not a small-ticket item you're talking about. This is *mucho dinero*, big bucks."

"You don't put—"

"—a price tag on human life. I know what you're saying." He took a spotless white handkerchief from his pocket and dabbed at beads of perspiration on his brow. "Bigger hospitals than this one have bankrupted themselves, trying to be all things to all people. To be honest, I'd rather see us lose a few nonessential services than go broke."

"And what do you consider nonessential?"

Smitson puckered his lips. "No you don't. I'm not falling into that trap. You're the chief of staff, the director of medical services; you decide."

"I think I've made my position clear. We get a lot of trauma patients—"

"Right. Damned fool tourists who think they can drive at freeway speeds on the Coastal Road and slam their cars into each other."

"We can't let people die."

"So we do our best to stabilize them and transfer them to a hospital that's better equipped to handle them. Other hospitals do it all the time."

"That's a cop-out."

"So? These are cost-intensive patients, and more than a few of them are uninsured. We've got an eighty-bed hospital, twenty of which are for extended care. Sixty beds, Wyatt, do not generate enough profit to support a frontline trauma unit."

"The hospital made a profit last year."

"Yes, and as administrator, it's my job to see that it continues to do so."

Wyatt resisted the temptation to remind Smitson that it had been he who had hired him. "I still think we can work something out."

Smitson held his hands palms up and peered skyward. "Is it going to rain money all of a sudden?"

"Maybe. I'll talk to my accountant and see what I can come up with."

Smitson's expression was skeptical. "Are you sure you want to do that? You've already sunk a lot of money in this place. I mean, there's such a thing as getting a return on your investment."

"Providing good medical care is return enough." Wyatt looked at his watch again. One-thirty. "Now you'll have to excuse me, I have an appointment."

"But—"

"Later," Wyatt said.

Eva Quintero glanced up as he came through the side door. "There you are. I was ready to send out a search party after you."

"That bad?" He shrugged off his suit jacket and pulled on a white lab coat. "I thought this afternoon's schedule was light."

"It *was*. Notice the past tense. Suffice it to say, it isn't anymore." She stood and picked up a small stack of charts, which she handed to him.

"It's that bad?"

"The examining rooms are filled, we're double-booked until four, you've got messages up to here"—

she gestured six inches above her head—"and there are two detail men who want to enlighten you about their respective company's latest wonder drug."

"What about Samantha Townsend? Is she here?"

Eva nodded. "In your office."

"I'll see her first," he said, flipping through the charts and skimming the messages attached.

"Mrs. Goldstein is in examining room one," she said, and raised her eyebrows. "You want her to wait?"

"I'll make it fast."

"Hmm. If she hears your voice, she'll be out here wanting to know why you aren't in with her already. She probably has her ear to the door now."

"Then I'll whisper." None of the messages were urgent, and he handed the charts back to Eva.

"I don't know why you just didn't hire Samantha in the first place," his office manager said. "All this interview business. The girl lives two houses down the street from you; you've known her since she was sixteen. You think she's an ax murderer or something?"

Eva never shied from speaking her mind. It was one of the things he liked best about her. "Not at all. I haven't seen her since she got home from college, and I want to make sure this is something she really wants to do. Taking care of an eight-year-old all summer isn't everyone's idea of having a good time."

"She's a very responsible young woman—"

"—whose mother volunteered her for the job," Wyatt finished for her. "I know what I'm doing, Eva."

"Uh-huh. If Mrs. Goldstein comes looking for you, I'm hiding under the desk."

He smiled and shook his head, then turned and started down the hall toward his office.

Three

Samantha Townsend was amazed at the smoothness of the skull. She touched it tentatively at first, aware that once upon a time, a brain had worked within the cranium, that eyes had gazed from those sockets, that the jaw—now wired shut—had opened to speak.

Who were you? she wondered, her fingers tracing the arch above the brow. How did you die?

She hesitated, then picked the skull up. It was lighter than she'd expected, but not at all fragile. Peering through the eye sockets, she could see the varying degrees of bone thickness.

Briefly she regretted not having taken that theater class as an elective in her junior year; it seemed fitting to quote a line from Hamlet at this point, would that she could only remember one.

Instead she cradled the back of the skull in the palm of her right hand and tilted it so she could examine it from another angle. As a film major, she'd been trained to value perspective above all else.

Behind her, the door opened. Startled, she felt the skull begin to fall from her grasp. She juggled it for a split second before getting a firm hold, her fingers slipping into the eye sockets.

She turned to face Dr. English, hiding the skull behind her back.

"Met Orville, have you?" he asked with a faint smile.

Samantha felt herself begin to blush and damned her Irish genes. "Orville?"

He nodded and came toward her, holding out his hands to accept the skull. She brought it slowly from behind her and watched his smile widen as he realized that she was holding Orville as if he were some kind of macabre bowling ball.

"Sorry," she said, handing him over and disengaging her fingers as gracefully as she could.

"He doesn't mind." Dr. English replaced the skull on the shelf. "He's tough."

Samantha decided against mentioning she'd almost dropped him.

"Have a seat."

"Absolutely." She went to sit in the chair opposite the desk, folding her hands in her lap to keep them from picking at a tear in her jeans.

She'd worn jeans today because Hansen's Point was a small town and working as a babysitter wasn't a power suit kind of job, but now she wished she'd dressed better. At least if she'd worn a nice pair of slacks, she'd have a crease to straighten.

"So, how is UCLA?"

"Educational." It was what she always said when anyone asked; until today she hadn't thought it sounded flippant. "But I'm glad to be home. Los Angeles in the summertime is not to be believed. Hot, smoggy, wall-to-wall traffic. But you know all that . . . you lived there, didn't you?"

He gave a slight nod. "Your mother tells me you might be going to London next year to finish your graduate studies?"

"Might be is right. I'm up for a scholarship which will cover the tuition and books, and the school provides a place to stay, but I have to come up with airfare and money for incidentals. Which is why I'm here."

Dr. English leaned back in his chair, regarding her with those remarkable dark blue eyes she remembered so well from the first time she'd ever seen him.

Wait a minute, she thought, don't get distracted.

She cleared her throat. "To be honest, I haven't had a lot of experience with kids, or at least not recently, not since I stopped baby-sitting when I got out of high school. But," she added determinedly, "it's gotta be like riding a bicycle. You never forget how. And I know I can handle it—"

A knock at the door interrupted her. "Excuse me for a moment," Wyatt said.

Samantha tried not to listen to the conversation being held in the doorway, but she couldn't help but notice the sense of urgency in Eva Quintero's tone of voice. She caught herself leaning in that direction, the better to hear. Their words were indecipherable. Across the room, Orville grinned at her.

"I'm sorry," Dr. English said, closing the door and turning to face her. "Something urgent has come up, and I have to go back to the hospital."

"Oh, sure, I understand." She stood.

"But I do want to talk to you—"

"I'm more than willing to wait, Dr. English. Or I can come back tomorrow."

"Better yet, why don't you stop by the house this evening? I'm usually home by seven or so. If I'm late, Mabel can show you around, and you can get reacquainted with Bronwyn."

"Sounds great." She smiled, hoping that he

41

wouldn't see her disappointment; she'd wanted to have the matter settled this afternoon, one way or the other. Preferably one way, as in being hired. "I'll see you then."

He held the door open for her, and she felt his hand on her back as he ushered her through.

"Oh," she said, as a question occurred to her. She pivoted to ask it, not realizing how close he was standing behind her. At this distance, she could drown in his eyes. Whatever question she'd had vanished in the space of a heartbeat.

"Yes?"

"Yes," she repeated, buying time, thinking madly. "Dr. English . . . would you like to see my résumé?" She winced as soon as the words were out of her mouth. What an incredibly dumb thing to say.

But he smiled. "I don't think that'll be necessary. You've got the job if you want it, Sam. Now I have to run," he said, and was gone, leaving her standing there, totally bemused.

Her mother had loaned her the car, but for some reason, Samantha didn't want to go home just yet. Instead she began to walk along Ocean Avenue, the town's main street. She saw her reflection in a succession of storefront windows and made faces at them all.

A few weeks back her roommates at UCLA had persuaded her, in a moment of weakness, to try one of the shorter, razor-cut hair styles. On the other girls, the style looked great, kind of punky, but sophisticated too.

On her . . . boy-scout chic. It warranted a merit badge for bravery, if nothing else.

Her mother had cried at the loss of her shoulder-length black hair, which had made *her* cry, although she'd done her crying later, in the privacy of her old bedroom.

"It'll grow out," her mother kept saying, and crossing herself, even though they weren't Catholic.

Samantha rubbed at the back of her neck; the short hair felt bristly and she couldn't imagine a man's hand caressing her—

"Hold it," she said out loud. What was she thinking? Whose hand was it that she had in mind? And why was she talking to herself?

A lady passing by gave her a curious look, apparently wondering as well.

The problem was, she knew the answers to what and who, and knowing bothered her.

Wyatt English was unquestionably devoted to his wife.

Everyone in town had heard the story, how he'd given up a promising medical practice in Los Angeles and had come to tiny Hansen's Point to find a place that would provide for her care.

The gossips had predicted initially that he was merely "passing through." He would leave her here, and return to the big city. After all, what did a small town have to offer him?

When that didn't happen, the consensus was that he would stay long enough to satisfy his conscience, but after a year or two, the urge to get on with his life would move him to abandon her.

Thereafter, they said, he would absolve himself of whatever guilt he had by paying the bills for her hospital care, and his marriage would be reduced to a function of bookkeeping, an item entered in a ledger.

The skeptics suggested that he might even divorce

43

her, if she lingered too long. At the very least, they agreed, it wouldn't surprise anyone if he took up with another woman. He was still a young man, good-looking, and had his entire life ahead of him. He needed a real wife, and a mother for his child. The time limit most frequently quoted for this eventuality was three years.

After the fourth year—about the time he acquired a fifty-one percent ownership of Point Hansen Hospital and had clearly settled in—talk began to circulate that Deborah English was in line for an inheritance, although no one could say from whom. Wyatt was standing by her, they said, in order to collect it, so that he could recoup what everyone agreed had to be extraordinary medical expenses.

No inheritance ever materialized.

Finally, during the summer of 1988, when none of the predictions had come true, the talkers began to argue among themselves as to which of them had always believed that Wyatt English was deeply in love with his wife, and would willingly give his own life if Deborah could be spared.

Samantha, who had listened to all of this and kept her own opinions private, felt vindicated.

She had known he wouldn't forsake his wife. One look in his eyes had convinced her of that.

It was so romantic that her throat ached, thinking of how it would end.

Now it was whispered around town that the end was near, that Deborah English was failing, and fast.

Felice, a friend of Samantha's from high school, had been working as an admitting clerk at the hospital, and she confirmed the whispers, saying that if Deborah survived through the summer, it would be nothing less than a miracle.

But no one should wish for that miracle, according to Felice, because it would be a blessing when Deborah English died.

"You should see her," Felice had said. "It's enough to break your heart."

Samantha had changed the subject. She didn't want to see Mrs. English in person, or hear the gruesome details of her decline. Samantha preferred to go on thinking of her as a sleeping beauty.

Like everyone else, she'd seen the pictures in Dr. English's office. They showed a pretty blond woman with come-hither hazel eyes. Her teasing smile held the hint of a challenge, but promised that the chase would be worth it . . . and unforgettable.

A heartbreaker, without question.

It was all so damned sad, but oh, what Samantha wouldn't give to be loved that intently, the way he loved her . . . it might be worth dying for.

She had reached the end of Ocean Avenue where it fronted the beach and she stopped, looking out at the undulating swell of waves. The fragrance of burning driftwood induced pangs of nostalgia.

As a child, she'd spent most of her summers on the beach, roasting hot dogs and marshmallows, drinking Pepsi from bottles slightly gritty with sand.

Her parents had lived together, and the word *divorce* had no meaning for her. She'd never thought in terms of being secure, but she had been.

Life had been so simple, and her memories of those summers never failed to bring a smile. Which was as it should be; childhood should be a special time.

She couldn't help but wonder what memories Bronwyn English would have.

Four

"Damn," Cassie Owens swore, looking at the schedule which was posted above the time clock. A series of neatly printed *W*'s were entered after her name.

She hated working the west wing, and would do anything to keep from being assigned duty there. Unfortunately, the nursing supervisors must have gotten together and compared notes, because lately her excuses had been falling on deaf ears.

Her next five shifts would be spent on West. All at once, Tuesday seemed an eternity away.

It wasn't only that the work was harder than on the medical or surgical wings—although no one could deny it was—but that being around the coma patients made her very, *very* uneasy.

There was something deeply unsettling about caring for a patient who never would respond.

Other nurses on the west wing contended that it was the silence that got on their nerves, but Cassie thought it was more than that.

A few years back, she'd spent two weeks as a private-duty nurse for an elderly man who was riddled with cancer and hovering near death. He was

47

heavily sedated, had undergone a tracheotomy at some point, and couldn't speak a word, but when she offered him comfort—a cool cloth for his forehead or chips of ice to melt on his tongue—his eyes thanked her.

The eyes of the patients on West were blank, empty, a frightening void.

And their eyes weren't even the worst of it.

"How were your days off?" a voice asked.

Cassie started; deep in thought, she hadn't heard anyone approach. "Excuse me?"

Annabeth Wilson, one of the aides, gave her a peculiar look. "I said, how were your days off?"

"Short and already forgotten."

"Boy, do I know the feeling." Annabeth selected her time card from the rack and inserted it in the clock, which gave a loud *thunk*. "Kind of like my paycheck, may it rest in peace." Annabeth laughed, a distinctive one-of-a-kind bray which generally elicited a similar response.

Cassie merely shook her head, feeling grim.

"What? Abject poverty doesn't even rate a smile anymore?"

"Sorry. I'm not in the mood to smile," Cassie said as they started down the hall toward the massive double doors which separated the administrative offices from the patient areas.

"Uh-oh. That bad?"

"I'm working West."

"Ugh, the zombie ward. I should have guessed. You have my sympathies."

"If it's all the same to you, I'd rather have your assignment." Cassie wasn't sure how it had come about, but Annabeth had managed to finagle a permanent place on the surgical floor.

Annabeth held one side of the door open for her

48

and smiled sweetly. "In your dreams."

"No," Cassie said, "my nightmares."

Usually Cassie detested sitting through Report, which often seemed to drag on and on as the charge nurse detailed each and every element of each and every patient's care, but today she wouldn't have minded if it lasted all shift. A minute spent in Report was one less minute she had to endure on the floor.

As luck would have it, however, old warhorse Rottweiler had the duty, and twenty years as an Army nurse had trained her not to waste words *or* time.

"Owens, you've got beds four, six, eight, and ten," Rottweiler said.

And that was pretty much it.

As she walked toward the nursing station, Cassie glanced at the photocopy of the census sheet to see who her patients were. Nakasone, English, Rath, and Perez. Of the four, only Perez was unknown to her from her last shift on West. The diagnosis on Perez was Coma, Status Post Head Injury.

More of the same, Cassie thought as she circled the room numbers of her patients. Another body with a scrambled brain.

When she reached the desk, the unit secretary handed her four charts, which on West were kept in binders rather than on clipboards. All four were thick, swollen with doctors' order sheets, lab test results, progress notes—although lack of progress would be a more accurate designation—and nursing continuation forms.

"Gee, thanks," Cassie said, plopping them onto the counter. "A little light summer reading. The problem is, I don't have all summer to read them. So why don't you tell me what's new?"

"It's been a while since you're pulled a shift here," the secretary said, "so you probably haven't heard, but it isn't going well for Deborah English."

Actually, she *had* heard—the hospital grapevine put Western Union to shame—but Cassie had learned the hard way to always listen to the secretaries, who were somehow privy to the medical equivalent of breaking news. So she said, "Oh?"

"They think she may be developing another case of pneumonia. Nothing shows up on the X rays yet, but she has a persistent low-grade fever and her most recent blood gas levels are borderline."

Cassie made a note to that effect on the census sheet and added a reminder to check the recent lab work on all of her charges.

"There are also signs," the secretary continued, lowering her voice to just above a whisper, "that her kidneys might be falling."

"Is the attending considering dialysis?"

"Not as far as I know."

Good, she thought, but felt it prudent not to say so. More and more she had come to disapprove of doctors who ordered extraordinary measures for patients who were clearly terminal.

"He *has* written an order for antibiotics," the secretary said, flipping the chart open unerringly to the page in question and tapping a manicured nail on the order sheet. "The day shift was supposed to begin giving the meds, but the IV infiltrated and they haven't been able to find a vein good enough to start a new one."

It was a common difficulty with long-term patients; over the years, their veins tended to collapse from repeated and extended use. The doctor could do a cutdown to find a vein not scarred from the endless rounds of intravenous lines and blood draws, but because of the possibility of infection, that would be done only as a last resort.

Which meant she would get to do the honors of sticking Deborah English however many times it took to establish a new line. Cassie had a knack with IVs, but the last time she'd done English, with her paper-thin veins, it had taken well over an hour.

"Shit," she said. "He couldn't order the meds to be given intramuscularly?"

"He could but he won't." The secretary gave her a sympathetic look. "Don't worry about it now. Her little girl's come for a visit, so you can probably put it off until after dinner."

"A reprieve," Cassie said, "is not the same as a pardon."

The first hour passed quickly enough, as Cassie took vital signs and suctioned the tracheal secretions of three of her four patients. Nakasone had soiled his bed and she went to the cart for fresh linens but found there were no clean gowns.

As she walked toward a second linen cart at the far end of the hall, she passed 6-West, and a flutter of movement caught her eye.

It was the child, Bronwyn, and she was dancing.

The rooms on West were all private, although none were particularly large, and there wasn't a great deal of open space; but the girl had found a clear spot in which she moved gracefully through a series of steps that looked to be ballet.

Cassie expected her to be humming or singing or even counting to herself, but she made not a sound. Was the child hearing the music in her mind?

51

For a minute, Cassie stood and watched.

The girl was slender, and small for an eight-year-old. Her features were delicate, those of a child destined for adult beauty. The rich blond color of her hair reminded Cassie of the butterscotch candies she'd loved when *she* was young.

She glanced from the child to the mother who lay as still as death in the bed.

Over the years, Cassie had heard from those who'd seen photographs that Bronwyn was the image of her mother as a child. The resemblance between them now, however, was not easily seen.

Deborah, eight years comatose, had wasted away to little more than a skeleton encased in skin. She weighed perhaps seventy-five pounds, and her muscle tone had atrophied, her tendons had shortened. Calcium deposits had tightened many of her joints.

Daily physical therapy—intensive for the therapist, passive for Deborah, and normally prohibitively expensive—had kept her from stricturing into the fetal position so common with these patients, but even if a miracle occurred tomorrow and she regained consciousness, it would be doubtful she'd ever be able to walk again.

Her hands were secured, using soft restraints, to cushioned armboards to prevent her fingers from contracting into misshapen claws.

Her jaw was in a lamb's-wool sling of sorts to keep her mouth from gaping open. She wore a clear plastic protective device over her upper and lower teeth to stop her from biting into her tongue.

A thin flesh-tone nasogastric tube was threaded through her nostril and down the back of her throat into her stomach. Several times a day, a nurse fed her a liquid formula—a powdery, chalky substance which had to be mixed with distilled water and smelled like hell—via the tube. Every other day, the tube was changed to prevent it from becoming blocked.

Although she wasn't reliant upon a respirator, she was hooked to a humidifier which added water vapor to the air she breathed. A tracheostomy had been performed for that purpose prior to her transfer, and the opening into her throat had to be suctioned frequently of the mucus which collected in the airway.

Beneath the covers, a catheter drained urine from her bladder. It, too, had to be changed frequently, because of the tendency of urine to crystallize within the tubing, and to forestall infections.

And then there were the gauze pads which were intended to keep the bony angles of her hips and knees and elbows from breaking through her skin. Bedsores—decubiti in the vernacular—were the bane of a nurse's existence. A tiny red spot on a pressure point could deteriorate into an open, angry wound seemingly within hours.

But beyond all of the medical aspects of Deborah as she was now, there was precious little left of the person she had once been.

If she'd shared that gorgeous shade of hair with her daughter, it was long gone. In fact, she hadn't much hair left at all; they kept it short for ease of washing it—long hair matted—and in her semimalnourished state, what they hadn't cut had thinned like an old woman's, and had darkened as well.

Her face, as seen between the tucks and folds of the jaw sling, might have been that of a cadaver. Her skin appeared gray but translucent, so that it was possible to see the fine network of blue and purple veins beneath it. There were deep furrows on either side of her mouth which might be called laugh lines, except that she hadn't laughed or smiled or frowned or cried or thought of doing such things in more than eight years.

Deborah was only thirty-four.

She had been twenty-six when it happened. Almost a quarter of her life had been passed in a coma.

Cassie's glance returned to the child, who had stopped her dance and now stood by the window. One hand was pressed against the glass, fingers spread wide. Her head was bowed, and soft waves of hair shielded her face from view.

It seemed to Cassie that the girl's body trembled. Was she crying as soundlessly as she'd danced?

Feeling like an intruder, Cassie hurried on.

Later she saw that the housekeeper had come for the child. Neither spoke as they passed the nursing station, but Cassie noticed that the little girl's eyes were slightly reddened.

Who could blame her?

Nevertheless, when their eyes met, she felt a twinge of unease.

Who do you blame? she wondered.

Five

"Please, Mrs. Henderson? It won't ruin my appetite, I promise."

"Your father doesn't want you to drink so much soda," Mabel Henderson said, as she did every time they had this discussion, which was every time they passed Alberti's Drug Store. Alberti's had an old-fashioned soda fountain, and their cherry Cokes were almost as good as those of years gone by.

Of course, back then cherry Cokes were served in tall iced glasses rather than paper cups, and the syrup had been added using a silver ladle instead of squirted from a tap. And the syrup foamed a bit—

"Then I'll order a small one," Bronwyn said, interrupting her reverie. The child looked up at her with those serious hazel eyes. "Please?"

Mabel sighed. "Oh, all right. But it had better be a small, and I'll expect you to finish your supper this evening without any prodding from me."

"I will."

"Hmm." Mabel dug down into the bottom of her purse where she let her loose coins collect. "I suspect you're taking advantage of me, child. And if your father hears of it—"

"He won't."

"—and I catch any grief, well, it'll be a while before you talk me into another cherry Coke." She selected five quarters from her change and dropped them in the child's outstretched hand.

Bronwyn smiled. "Thank you."

Mabel watched after her as she ducked into the drug store and made a beeline for the fountain in the back. A little wisp of a girl, she had to stand tiptoe to be seen over the counter. When she'd given her order to the clerk, she turned and waved at Mabel.

Heavens, but she would miss that child this summer.

Last night, after she'd tucked her into bed, she'd gone to Dr. English and offered to postpone her vacation, but he wouldn't hear of it.

"I'm not sure how we'll manage without you, Mabel," he said, "but you have to take some time off. Every year there's been one reason or another why you didn't feel you could take vacation and leave us to our own devices, but this time I insist."

"I'm concerned, Dr. English, that I won't be here when she needs me." She'd hesitated, not wanting to put into words what she'd been thinking. "If . . . if the time has come . . ."

"I don't know that it has."

She hadn't had the heart to contradict him, but they both knew better. And the strain of knowing showed in the set of his mouth, and in a heavy weariness that seemed to settle over him in the evenings. Who was she to add to his burden?

If anything, she wished to lighten it. If only she knew how.

Wyatt English was a private man who held his feelings inside. In the years that she'd been working for him, she'd never seen him despair when things

56

were going bad, nor truly rejoice when life was good.

Mabel wondered if it was healthy to maintain equanimity under the circumstances. She wasn't a demonstrative woman by any means, but sometimes she wished that just once he would lose his temper and damn the unfairness of what he and his daughter had been through.

The door to the drug store opened, and Bronwyn came out, drinking her cherry Coke through two thin straws. Her expression was one of bliss.

"Good, is it?" Mabel asked.

Bronwyn nodded.

Mabel brushed a strand of blond hair back from the child's face, tucking it behind her ear. "Then let's be on our way."

They walked slowly, out of deference to her arthritis and the beauty of the day, but even so they made it home before five. Late afternoon sunlight slanted through the narrow windows on either side of the door, but there wasn't a dust mote that'd dare dance in its rays, not in her pristine hallway.

Bronwyn excused herself and disappeared upstairs to change out of her school clothes.

Mabel went directly to the kitchen and lifted the glass lid off the slow cooker. The chicken she was simmering in a white wine sauce smelled delicious, and when she put the fork to it, the meat fell away from the bones.

She busied herself at her chores, setting the table in the kitchen for Bronwyn's and her own dinner, and a solitary place in the dining room for his. He seldom made it home before six-thirty or seven, which was too late to be making a child wait to eat.

She rinsed salad greens in cold water and tossed

them with a dash of vinaigrette. She put the crusty loaf of sourdough bread she'd gotten fresh from the baker in the oven to warm.

That done, she went into her small suite of rooms at the back of the house to see about finishing her packing. Because the nearest airport was an hour's drive away, she had to make an early start in the morning in order to catch an eleven A.M. flight.

If indeed, she didn't change her mind and decide to stay . . .

Promptly at half-past five she called Bronwyn to dinner. As promised, the child ate well, cleaning her plate and even asking for a second helping.

Mabel spooned the chicken—it was that tender— onto the plate and watched as Bronwyn took a bite. For an eight-year-old, she had lovely table manners. But then, she'd been *taught* them; so many adults mistakenly assumed that manners accumulated with age and not effort, thus never bothering to instruct their children.

There were, in her estimation, at least two generations whose eating habits were abominable, to put it mildly. Which reminded her . . .

"While I'm gone," Mabel said, "you're to eat at the table, and not in front of the television."

Bronwyn looked surprised, as though the thought had never occurred to her.

Which, Mabel realized, it probably hadn't.

"And no snacking." She folded her linen napkin and placed it on the table beside her plate before rising. "Just because I won't be here doesn't mean that there aren't any rules."

"I know," Bronwyn said. "I know the rules."

"I want you to . . . to behave. No running wild,

you hear me? I don't want to have to civilize you all over again when I get back."

"Yes, ma'am."

"I've written my sister's number on the message board by the kitchen phone, and you can call me there collect if you need anything."

Bronwyn's smile lit up the room. Gazing at that sweet little face, Mabel wanted to gather the child to her and keep her from harm.

Was it possible to kiss away the hurt of losing a mother?

She felt a lump begin to form in her throat and she looked away. "Now finish up," she said when she could trust her voice not to break. "The young lady your father's hired to watch over you will be over soon, and you'll want to say hello to her."

She'd hoped to talk to Dr. English privately before Samantha Townsend arrived, but the two of them showed up at the same time. Had the girl been lurking in the bushes, waiting for him to come home?

Mabel stood aside, holding the door open for them, and trying not to glare.

"Hi, Mrs. Henderson," Samantha said, and had the grace to blush.

My, but didn't she look young? And what on earth had she done to her hair? "Samantha. It's nice to see you. How's your mother?"

"Fine, thanks." She hesitated. "I hope it's all right that I'm early."

"Well . . ." It should be obvious, Mabel thought, that by being early she was delaying dinner. She was on the verge of saying so when Dr. English spoke.

"No problem at all." He favored her with a smile

as he shrugged out of his jacket and glanced at his watch. "I made you wait for half an hour this afternoon—I owe you thirty minutes."

Mabel took note of the look Samantha gave him. So, she still had a crush on him. Not that *that* was much of a surprise.

"We can talk in the library," Dr. English said, handing her the jacket to hang up. "If you'll excuse us, Mrs. Henderson?"

There was nothing to say, so she simply nodded, folding the jacket over her arm and watching them walk down the hall, Samantha a few paces behind.

It took all the willpower she could muster to keep from going straight to the phone, calling the airline and canceling her flight.

Six

Percy Smitson ran his left index finger along a column of figures while with his right hand, he entered the numbers on the adding machine. At least six feet of paper tape curled from the machine onto his desk. The wastebasket beside the desk was full to overflowing with similar lengths of tape.

There were those in the business office who considered his reliance on an adding machine archaic, or perhaps worse, eccentric. The computer system which produced the hospital's financial data didn't make mistakes, they said.

Neither did he.

The difference between his own work and the computer's was that he trusted himself. The computer? It was overrated as far as he was concerned, and far too vulnerable in these days of viruses and illegal access.

As administrator, he needed to be invulnerable. It was his job.

He was responsible for overseeing every aspect—big or small—of running the hospital. He was the one who would be held accountable if its performance was not satisfactory on any level, but of course the emphasis had to be on the bottom line.

Point Hansen Hospital was a business, pure and simple. As a business, it had to make a profit to survive. To make a profit required that costs not exceed income.

It could hardly get more basic than that.

Percy hit the total bar, and listened to the whir of the adding machine as it tallied the numbers. The result was identical to the computer's.

He made a tiny check mark on the paper tape and entered the results in the over-sized ledger which he preferred to the unwieldy spread sheets Accounting was so fond of. He gathered up the computer printouts and dumped them into his out basket.

Done at last.

And the news was good; with the end of the fiscal year rapidly approaching—and barring any unforeseen expenses—the hospital was solidly, securely in the black. For the third year running, he'd brought it off.

Leaning back in his custom-built chair, he indulged himself in a moment of self-congratulation which he felt he thoroughly deserved.

All across the country, hospitals were going under, burdened by spiraling expenses at a time when Medicare and the major insurers were implementing stringent cost-containment measures. Patients were discharged according to a timetable, with the length of stay determined by the admitting diagnosis.

The powers that be had apparently determined that all myocardial infarctions were created equally, and that the course of one man's acute gastroenteritis or nephritis was indistinguishable from another's. There was little allowance made for those who were slow to recover.

Assembly-line medicine. Even with his own respect for profit margins, he questioned the methods behind the insurers' madness.

As if that weren't trouble enough, there was also a nationwide shortage of nurses. Nursing schools were closing, and the work permits of the foreign nurses who'd been recruited to fill the gap between supply and demand were expiring.

He himself had been forced to devise an incentive package—higher salaries, flexible hours, bonuses, handsome shift differentials, and even moving-expense reimbursement—in order to fulfill the hospital's rather modest staffing requirements.

The only surplus these days was in lawyers looking to sue hospitals and doctors for malpractice or negligence or for the hell of it.

The health-care industry was in crisis, but *his* hospital was doing okay.

He meant to keep it that way.

As for Wyatt English's plan to upgrade the facilities in Emergency to handle trauma patients, well, it just wouldn't fly. The thought of all that capital outlay—which would put them in the red—made him cringe.

No, it wouldn't fly. If necessary, he'd manufacture a crisis on paper, shift funds, inflate operating costs, or do whatever it took to keep control.

Percy sighed. Doctors. He wouldn't attempt to perform an appendectomy; why did they feel free to intrude on his domain?

He stood, reached across the desk to switch off the green-shaded Banker's lamp, and was momentarily surprised by how dark the room became. He pressed a button on his watch to illuminate the display.

Twelve minutes after eight.

His hour of extra work had stretched into three. "Oh well," he said. "Another day, another dollar." Minus, of course, federal and state withholding tax, SSI, disability, and the automatic payment to the credit union on his car loan.

After locking his office, Percy decided to take a tour through the hospital and check things out. The evening shift tended to slow down after the paper pushers left, and it'd do them good to come upon him roaming the halls.

The administration offices were long since deserted, and he encountered no one until he reached the south wing, which housed both the fifteen-bed Surgical Unit, and the Critical Care Unit's ten beds.

He walked slowly but purposefully, the better to see and be seen. Some things shouldn't be rushed, and besides, it wasn't as though anyone was waiting for him at home; he lived alone.

As he neared the nursing station on Surgical, he sensed a ripple of awareness pass among the nurses who were gathered there. All eyes were upon him.

"Evening," he said. He was close enough to see that most were working on their charting, but one old gal had an open magazine in front of her, and she made no attempt to disguise the fact that she'd been reading.

Percy looked pointedly from the offender to the magazine and back at her again. Her name tag identified her as an R.N., which meant she should know better. "A slow night?" he asked.

"Praise the Lord, yes," she said.

He blinked, taken aback. Was it possible she didn't know who he was? He drew himself up to his full height, ready to enlighten her.

On the master panel, a buzzer sounded and a blue light came on. Down the hall, a corresponding light began to flash outside one of the rooms. A nurse and two of the aides got up to answer the call, *en masse*, apparently not wanting to hang around.

A look from him stopped all but one of them dead in their tracks. The nurse, pulling rank, hurried off.

"If," he said, so quietly they had to lean forward to hear him, "you haven't enough work to keep you busy, I can rectify that."

Still not getting it, the old nurse simply shook her head and smiled.

Percy counted silently to ten. He reminded himself that nurses were a precious resource. He reminded himself that the nurse's union was sniffing around, looking for a way in. He reminded himself that at the hospital where he'd worked before Point Hansen, a situation much like this had triggered a long and bitter labor relations dispute over the professional integrity of nurses, whatever the hell *that* was.

The dispute had been instrumental in hastening his own departure from that hospital. . . .

But how could he overlook this? It was a direct affront to his authority.

"Perhaps you'd care to finish your shift on West?"

"Oh, heavens no."

"Well, we have to do something." To his own ears, he sounded like the very voice of reason and restraint. "The hospital isn't"—he meant *I'm* not—"paying you to sit and read *Redbook*."

The nurse tilted her head in a peculiar birdlike gesture, as if to say Why not?

Damn, but he wished he'd been around in the days when nurses were little more than chattel, or handmaids to the doctors. No doubt, he thought, she had been. Was this her revenge?

Percy cleared his throat, and had opened his mouth to speak, before it came to him that he was balanced on the edge of a precipice. There was a palpable atmosphere of hostility which he'd be a fool to disregard. He was, he realized, in an untenable position. Whatever he said or did, someone would take offense.

All at once, it was quiet enough to hear a pin drop.

Belatedly, he closed his mouth, feeling absurdly like a fish caught out of water.

The only possible answer, as he saw it, was not to say another word. And the solution was clipped to his belt. For once, it was a blessing to be short, because the counter came nearly chest high on him, and he was in part hidden from view. As surreptitiously as he could, he reached beneath his coat and fumbled for a moment before finding and activating the test button on his beeper.

He arranged his face in a scowl, as though irritated at the interruption, then pulled the beeper off his belt and held it up, lest they miss the implication: he was being called away, and *not* running off with his tail between his legs.

"Excuse me," he said.

The silence followed him off the wing.

He skipped the Critical Care unit and Maternity—pregnant women made him nervous and squalling babies made his teeth ache—and headed for the west wing.

There was a little matter of some electrical problems they'd been having on West that he might as well attend to while he had it in mind.

Earlier today he'd gone through the Incident Reports for the month of May and on a whim had separated the reports into two sections; one for those incidents relating to nursing care—failure to put up bed rails or an unsupervised patient falling out of bed—and the other regarding equipment malfunctions.

Oddly, and contrary to his expectations, there were

66

significantly more in the second category than the first. Even more curious was the fact that seven out of nine of the equipment incidents reported had taken place on the west wing.

That had driven him to request and look through other such files for prior months. For some reason he'd never noticed it, but there was undeniably a pattern. The ratio of cases since the beginning of the year had remained constant.

There was an explanation for that, he suspected. The patients on West were machine dependent, and their rooms were equipped with all the sophisticated gadgetry that the biomedical engineers could come up with.

The equation was simple: the more machines in use, the more machines that could fail.

The expense of purchasing and maintaining all of the technology was not inconsiderable, but these patients were largely the victims of accidents. As such, they were beneficiaries of awards and settlements which more than compensated for their medical care.

One of the recent arrivals had been awarded twelve-point-two million dollars after a head-on auto accident rendered his brain to, roughly, the equivalent of vegetable soup. The defendants had included not only the other driver, but the manufacturer of the patient's car, the designer of the seat belts, and the county in which the accident occurred, whose safety engineer had failed to recommend a passing lane on a blind curve.

These patients were not only the hospital's bread and butter, they were its life's blood.

And although some of them had brought about their own misfortune—motorcyclists, primarily—he regarded them fondly.

He wouldn't want to see anything happen to any of them as a result of equipment failure.

There was no one at the nursing station, but he followed the sound of voices and found everyone crowded into 10-West. The patient, a male, was laid out flat on his back. He was naked, and seemed to have tubes and wires coming from everywhere.

Percy stood in the doorway and watched. Over the years he'd witnessed dozens of codes, but they never failed to fascinate him.

A backboard had been placed beneath the man, and one of the nurses was perched on the bed beside him, giving him the cardio part of cardiopulmonary resuscitation while a respiratory technologist forced air into his lungs using a small portable ventilator.

The nurse doing the cardiac compressions stopped for a few seconds while the doctor plunged a wicked-looking needle into the man's chest, aiming, Percy knew, directly for the heart.

"Five milligrams epinephrine," the doctor said a moment later as he withdrew the needle. A pinpoint of blood welled from the puncture wound.

"Still straight-line," a second nurse reported.

"Resume CPR."

The first nurse, red-faced from exertion, positioned her hands over the sternum and took up where she'd left off. Even from a distance Percy could see drops of sweat rolling down her face and dropping from her nose and chin onto the patient.

How unsanitary, he thought, but then, that was the least of this patient's problems.

"Calcium chloride on board," another voice said.

"Give another milligram of atropine," the doctor said. His eyes were fixed on the cardiac monitor where the rhythm of the heart, as aided by CPR, was displayed.

"Atropine on board."

"Stop CPR," the doctor ordered. "Let's see what we've got here."

Percy looked with the rest of them. The green line on the monitor went straight.

"Ah, shit," the doctor said. He leaned across the patient and pulled up the left eyelid, using a penlight to flash a beam into the eye. He flicked the beam away and back. Then he checked the right eye. "Pupils are fixed and dilated. How long has it been?"

"Forty-five minutes," someone answered.

"That's it, then."

The respiratory tech disconnected the ventilator from the tube which extended from the patient's mouth. The nurse who'd done CPR got down off the bed and accepted a paper towel to wipe her face.

The doctor accepted a chart the unit secretary handed him, glanced at his watch, and wrote down the time of death.

One of the other nurses switched off the cardiac monitor and began to peel the adhesive-backed electrodes off the man's chest. Another turned off the flow of IV fluid and set about removing the needles.

Percy took a last hard look at the man before they covered him up. Perez, he thought, a recent transfer from Sonoma. If memory served, he'd been thrown from a horse on his wealthy family's estate. He'd landed on his head, and the horse had trod on him in its panic.

A pity, Percy thought.

It was early in the course of his coma; he ought to have been good for a lot of money.

Seven

Samantha listened to Mrs. Henderson detail the house rules and thought she felt a headache coming on. For at least ten minutes—without doubt the longest ten minutes of her life—she'd been nodding and murmuring ackowledgment of the housekeeper's instructions, with what she hoped was an interested smile on her face.

And it was beginning to get to her.

"Bronwyn has her dance lessons on Mondays and Fridays," the older woman said. "Class starts at four, but I try to have her there at least fifteen minutes early so that she can warm up properly."

"Fifteen minutes," Sam said.

"Yes. The teachers don't always give the girls time enough to stretch."

"I see."

"Then when class is over, you should bring her straight home so she can have a bath—"

"A bath, of course."

"You'll want to fix her a light dinner on those evenings so that she doesn't become nauseated."

"A light dinner, yes," Samantha said, trying not to laugh. The way she was parroting the housekeeper's

71

instructions, she was tempted to say *Bronwyn wants a cracker?*

"Soup is good," Mrs. Henderson said, "or if it's a warm night, perhaps a fruit salad or yogurt."

Bronwyn, who'd been listening in silence throughout, wrinkled her nose. "Yogurt."

For an eight-year-old, she managed to convey her disdain quite well. Sam had never acquired a taste for the stuff herself, and she winked knowingly at Bronwyn.

Mrs. Henderson, thank God, missed it.

Dr. English, who'd left them while he went to his office to take a call from the hospital, chose that moment to return. "About done?" he asked.

"Yes," Sam answered before Mrs. Henderson could. "I think I've got the gist of it."

"Good." He placed a hand on his daughter's head. "It's your bedtime, young lady."

"Do I have to? Tomorrow's the last day of school—"

"You have to."

Bronwyn folded her arms across her chest in a huff; but then her father bent down and hugged her to him, and the disappointment went out of her eyes. Sam smiled, genuinely this time, and watched as they started for the stairway hand in hand.

"I'll be down in a minute," Dr. English called to her over his shoulder, "and walk you home."

"You don't have to do that."

"Humor me," he said.

Mrs. Henderson bustled off somewhere—Sam pictured her checking the expiration dates on coupons or something equally organized—and she wandered over to the stereo to see what kind of music

72

the doctor liked.

The compact discs were displayed in a small wood-and-glass case on a shelf above the stereo. Some of the artists represented came as a surprise: Fine Young Cannibals, Simply Red, Terence Trent D'Arby, Mr. Mister. . . .

It was good music, nothing radical—she had several of the same albums—but it wasn't at all what she thought he'd choose. He had to be in his late thirties; shouldn't he be listening to the old Beatles stuff and that other sixties music?"

"Sam, Sam, Sam," she chided herself. "Aren't you being a little bit of a snob?"

A lot of her college friends were annoyed when adults—meaning people with jobs and kids and mortgages—latched on to *their* music. As though being a parent left you tone deaf and hopelessly out of sync. Or doddering, to use a word her roommates favored.

Wyatt English wasn't any of those things. In some ways, he was younger than she.

She would never forget the night of her junior prom.

It had been unusually hot during the day, and she had cut her sixth-period biology class and come home early, ostensibly to get ready for the dance. But the heat made her languid, and after her shower she'd drawn the shades and lain down in her silk slip.

Behind the shades, she'd left the windows open so that the ocean breezes that came up every afternoon when the sun began to set would cool the house. The freshening air would wake her if she overslept.

The breezes arrived with the twilight, but though they caressed her, chilling her damp skin, it was the sound of voices that roused her from an uneasy sleep.

At first she thought it was her mother, home from

73

her job at the telephone exchange. Samantha sat up drowsily, and brushed her hair back from her face.

"Mom?" she called, still in a daze.

There was no answer. She realized then that the voices were coming from outside.

As if in a dream she got up and went to the window. Standing in the shadows so she couldn't be seen, she watched as Bronwyn, in diapers and a T-shirt, learning to walk at age one, tottered across the yard toward her father, who apparently had just arrived home.

He was dressed in a suit, but he took off his jacket and handed it and his briefcase to the housekeeper who was standing on the front steps of the house, then started in his daughter's direction.

"Come on, sweetie," he said, voice carrying in the stillness. "Come to Daddy."

Bronwyn veered off suddenly, heading for the sprinklers on the neighbor's lawn, running as fast as her plump little legs could go.

Wyatt raced after her, laughing as he scooped her up just inches from where the water arced. And then he stepped deliberately into the path of the sprinkler, getting both of them wet.

Bronwyn's delighted laughter echoed through the neighborhood. She squirmed to be let down, and her father obliged, but he continued to stand there, getting more drenched by the minute, while she investigated the sprinkler head.

From her hidden vantage point, Samantha smiled. The waning light faded quickly, making it difficult to see them, but she stood and watched until they went inside.

Somehow, after that, the paper lanterns and floral decorations at the prom didn't seem as enchanting as she'd thought they'd be. Nor was the forbidden

74

champagne she sipped later that night as tantalizing as fantasies she'd begun to—

"Sam?"

She jumped, startled nearly out of her skin. "I'm sorry," she said, wondering if her expression revealed the nature of her thoughts. "I was daydreaming."

"A nice night for it," Wyatt said, glancing past her to the opened terrace doors. "Smells like rain. Are you ready?"

Samantha nearly said For what?, but held her tongue. Instead she nodded. "My mother'll send out the National Guard if I'm not home soon."

He raised an eyebrow. "How's she going to handle your living here for two months?" he asked as they went out the door and down the front steps.

"Well, from our upstairs we've got a pretty good view of your place, and if I know her, she'll be digging out the binoculars, just to keep an eye on things."

"I doubt she'll be alone in that," he said wryly.

They had reached the sidewalk and she stopped, turning to look at him in the dim light of the streetlamps. "What do you mean?"

He seemed hesitant, but after a moment said, "You're an attractive young woman."

That was all, but Samantha immediately understood the implications of what he'd said—or rather, was not saying—and she didn't like it one bit.

"You think they'll think that we . . ." She couldn't bring herself to finish the question, although it was dangerously close to what *she'd* been thinking.

"I imagine they will." He regarded her seriously. "I personally don't give a damn what anyone thinks or says about me—"

"You *know* what they say about you?" she interrupted. It had never occurred to her that he'd be aware that he was being talked about. She would have thought he was above even noticing the petty gossip endemic in a small town like Hansen's Point.

"Of course. But what I wanted to say is, if it's going to make you uncomfortable, living in the house with us, I'm sure we can work it out so you can stay at home. You live so close—"

"Forget it," she said. "If you don't care what they say, neither do I."

"You're sure about that?"

"Absolutely." Samantha lifted her chin in defiance. "I stopped worrying about what the neighbors think years ago." It wasn't entirely true, and quite possibly her motives weren't pristine, but right now she was mad enough not to care.

"All right, but if you change your mind . . ." He left the rest unsaid.

"Not likely."

They resumed walking. Samantha, quietly fuming, sneaked a sideways glance at him, wondering how he always seemed to keep his cool.

But then, what was the idle chatter of small-minded, big-mouthed people to him?

Or to her?

She hoped that there *were* eyes watching from behind the curtains of the houses along the street. She hoped they noticed that his hand occasionally brushed against hers as they walked.

And she fervently hoped that if anyone had anything to say, they'd say it to her, because she hadn't lived most of her life in this town without learning a few of *their* little secrets.

There were glass houses all around them . . . and she had a supply of stones.

Eight

Bronwyn sat in the window seat, arms hugging her pajamaed knees to her chest, and looked out at the dark and silent neighborhood.

Several times this week she'd awakened at night, long after the house had grown still, and had risen from her bed to sit and breathe the fresh air. Outside, the crickets sang, interrupted at intervals by the eerie wavering call of a night bird.

The bird sounded lonesome to her.

Being lonely was something Bronwyn understood; she was often lonely, even when she wasn't alone. She suspected from the look in his eyes that her father was, too.

She'd given it a lot of thought these last few nights, and it had come to her that she and her father were filled up with sadness, the way a jar filled with rain if you left it out in a storm, and that the sadness didn't leave much room for anything else.

Not that they sat around crying all the time—she'd never seen him cry, and she tried not to because she was eight and big girls didn't—but some times when she was trying to be happy, at school or even at dance class, she couldn't do it.

No one had told her how.

Oh, she played like the other kids, and laughed and smiled, but that was pretending; the feeling inside never changed.

Bronwyn sighed and leaned forward, pressing her face against the soft mesh screen. The faintly dusty smell of the screen tickled her nose, and she waited for a sneeze which didn't come.

Somewhere in the distance, a dog barked, joined a second later by another. Probably, she thought, they were barking at the skunks which were a familiar sight on the outskirts of town. And, lately, even *in* town.

Last Saturday when she and Mrs. Henderson walked to the hospital to visit her mother, they'd come upon a dead skunk in the middle of the road. Bronwyn had covered her mouth and nose with her hand, just in case, but it had been dead long enough that the smell had faded.

A big black bird—a crow, she guessed—was picking at the raw red meat from when a car had run the skunk over and split it open. The crow spread its wings, as though standing guard over its feast, but otherwise ignored them as they walked by.

"Come on, now," Mrs. Henderson had urged her, but she had glanced back over her shoulder, sick with fascination. The bird was hopping almost comically, pulling at a strip of flesh.

A car turned onto the street and the bird flew off, but only momentarily, returning to the skunk as soon as the car had passed. Its beak poked and prodded, and this time it came away with a small chunk. The crow tossed its head back and, making gulping motions, swallowed the piece of skunk whole.

They had reached the corner and soon were out of

view. On the way home, they took a different street.

Although the housekeeper didn't say so, Bronwyn knew that it was death Mrs. Henderson didn't want her to be witness to.

That was odd because, as a doctor's daughter, there wasn't any way to avoid it. People died all of the time. Her father didn't talk to her directly about the deaths, but she knew just the same.

Just as she knew that something was about to happen with her mother. She wasn't sure why, but she had a sense that the waiting was nearing an end.

And every so often, for no reason that she knew of, the hair on Bronwyn's arms would rise and a chill would tingle up her spine.

Soon, she thought. Soon.

Friday

Nine

June 15th

Wyatt arrived at the hospital before six A.M. and headed directly for the west wing. The lights in the halls were still dimmed and the day shift had yet to arrive, but the day's activities were already under way.

Carts containing clean linens or packaged, sterile medical supplies were being distributed to the floors. Soon they would be followed by those from the kitchens with the breakfast trays.

The night secretary from admitting, delivering the daily census reports, stifled a yawn and then smiled at him as she passed.

Two of the maintenance engineers stood in the middle of the hallway, thumbs characteristically hooked in their tool belts, and staring up at the ceiling where a missing panel revealed a series of pipes and ducts overhead.

"Whatta ya think?" one asked the other.

"Big fucking termites," the second replied before he noticed that they weren't alone. He grinned sheepishly. "Oh . . . hi, Doc."

"Good morning," Wyatt said.

They returned to their contemplation of the ceiling and he continued on toward West, followed a moment later by the sound of their laughter. Maybe, he thought, that was a good omen to start the day.

In his experience, mornings were a time of cautious optimism in the hospital. For those caring for the gravely ill, there was a sense of having gotten through another night. Fevers often broke with the coming of dawn. And the three A.M. terrors that were the basis for so many cries in the dark were forgotten by day.

There was something innately reassuring about the sun rising in the morning.

He reached the entrance to West and paused briefly—as he always did—before pushing open the double doors which were kept closed between midnight and seven. His footsteps preceded him down the hall.

A glance at the nurses on duty, who looked up as he approached, told him that Deborah had made it through yet another night.

Wyatt leaned down and kissed his wife on the cheek, then brushed her hair back and laid his hand on her forehead. Her skin was cool and dry to the touch.

He noticed that her eyelashes were crusted with dried lacrimal secretions—or "sleep," as Bronwyn called it. He went into the small private bathroom, found a clean washcloth and held it under the faucet until the water finally ran warm. After wringing out the washcloth, he returned to the bedside.

Gently, he washed Deborah's closed eyes and then her face. He washed around the brace she wore, and

84

beneath the nasogastric tube, discovering in the process that the tape meant to secure the tube had come loose. He removed the tape and threw it away.

He located a roll of hypoallergenic tape in the drawer of the table by the bed and tore off a four-inch length. He deftly crisscrossed it once around the tube, then smoothed the tape into a V, with one end running across her upper lip and the other up and over the bridge of her nose.

With a practiced eye, he examined the connection from the humidifier to the tracheostomy site, and scanned the digital displays of the monitoring equipment, satisfying himself that everything was in order.

Then he bent down a second time. "I love you," he whispered into her ear.

After leaving West he made his rounds, checking on the progress of his patients before heading to the office for his morning appointments.

The young soldier with meningitis had shown little improvement, but his temperature was down and Wyatt expected that the antibiotic would kick in soon. He ordered a blood test for electrolytes, to determine if an imbalance existed due to dehydration, and left instructions that he wanted to be notified when the results were in.

The next patient, Gladys Hornsby, was waiting for him, dressed and sitting on the bed with her suitcase all packed beside her. Looking at her, it was hard to believe that this was the same eighty-two-year-old woman who, when he'd admitted her with a severe case of the flu on Monday, had been too ill even to sign her name.

"Gladys," he said, taking her frail, blue-veined

hand in both of his and patting it. "I take it you're ready to go home?"

"No, honey, I was fixing to elope." Her pale gray eyes were full of mischief.

"Anyone I know?" he asked.

"How about yourself?"

Wyatt smiled. "I'm honored, Gladys, but you know I'm a married man."

"Oh my!" Twin spots of red appeared high on her cheeks, and she looked flustered. "I'm so sorry, Wyatt. Sometimes my mouth gets away from me and I don't know what on earth I'm saying."

"Don't worry—"

"What must you think of me, saying such a thing, and with your poor wife . . . oh, what was I thinking of? I am an old fool."

"Not at all."

"Alzheimer's disease, that's what it is. My brain is shrinking like a bitter nut in a shell. A tiny, shriveled, bitter nut."

"Hush," he said firmly. "Your brain is fine, and you're a lovely lady, and if I took offense every time anyone said anything that reminded me of Deborah, I'd be in a perpetual state of pique . . . but I'm not."

"Even if that's true, it was an insensitive thing for me to say." Now she gathered his hands in hers, and squeezed them with surprising strength. "I pray for you and your family every Sunday."

Wyatt knew that what she prayed for was an end to his "ordeal." How could he thank her for her prayers when he still held onto a thread of hope?

How could he thank her when what she was praying for was for Deborah to die?

Finally, at a loss for words, he merely nodded.

Ten

The changing of the guard, as Samantha had come to think of it, was scheduled to occur at eight o'clock sharp. Or in military jargon—since Mrs. Henderson reminded her of the drill sergeants in those old blood-and-guts war movies—at oh eight hundred hours.

She left the house at a quarter to, but by the time she'd walked ten yards, she realized that wearing shorts at this early hour might not have been the best of ideas. It was cooler out than the brilliant blue sky had led her to expect.

The wind had a bite to it, and her bare legs prickled with gooseflesh.

She hesitated, wondering if she should go back inside and change into something warmer. If she did, she ran the risk of being late.

That wouldn't do, Samantha decided, so she hurried on. This morning's plan was for her to walk Bronwyn to school, then come back for a final debriefing before Mrs. Henderson left for the airport. Maybe the walk would warm her up.

Or, failing that, maybe Mrs. Henderson would give her one of those blistering looks. . . .

She made it to the English house with not a

moment to spare, arriving just as Bronwyn and the housekeeper stepped out onto the porch. "Good morning. A beautiful day, isn't it?"

Mabel Henderson narrowed her eyes at the sky and sniffed. "Rain's coming."

"It is? In June?"

"By nightfall," Mrs. Henderson affirmed.

"Hmm." There wasn't a cloud in sight. If it *did* rain and catch her unprepared, it wouldn't be the first time; she was forever finding herself stranded without an umbrella in a downpour. "Well, what will be, will be."

Mrs. Henderson gave her a sour look.

Sam hunkered down so that she was face-to-face with Bronwyn. "And how are you this morning?"

"It's the last day of school," the child said by way of a reply.

"So you're great then, I'd guess." Samantha straightened and turned to see the housekeeper giving her the once-over. She tugged at her shorts, which weren't *that* short, as unobtrusively as she could. "Well, we'd better be on our way."

"Bronwyn," Mrs. Henderson said, "you remember all of the things I told you."

"Yes'm."

"And be a good girl for your father." Her tone was gruff but her eyes glistened.

Amazingly, Samantha felt a pang of sympathy for the older woman, whose chin and mouth were trembling from the effort of holding back tears. She gave Bronwyn a gentle nudge forward, and watched as the child was gathered in for a hug.

Mabel Henderson kissed the top of the little girl's head, and then rested her cheek on the silken blond hair, closing her eyes tightly.

Sam looked away, not wanting to intrude on a private moment, and feeling guilty about her uncharitable thoughts toward the housekeeper.

However regimented Mrs. Henderson was, she obviously cared for the child.

That had to count for something.

"So, what do you want to do this summer?" Sam asked when they'd reached the end of the street.

Bronwyn tilted her head and gave Sam a sidelong glance. "Do?"

"You know, for fun."

"Oh." She frowned, considering. "Well, there's my dance class—"

"Right, I've got it." Sam ticked the items off on her fingers. "Warm-ups, dancing lessons, a bath, and a light dinner. What else?"

"I don't know."

"You must do *something* else for fun," she said, even though she could see the kid was clearly perplexed. "Go to the beach? Build sand castles?"

That brought a response, although not what Sam had anticipated.

"Can I really?" Bronwyn asked wistfully.

"Of course . . . Haven't you ever been to the beach?"

"No."

Sam blinked, surprised. The locals weren't as beach crazy as the tourists—a case of familiarity breeding not contempt but indifference—but you just didn't live in a beach town and not go to the beach at least once in a while. "Never?"

"Maybe when I was a baby, but I don't remember it. My dad's awful busy."

"Sure he is, but couldn't someone else take you?"

"No one did."

They stopped at a street corner and waited for the light to change. "I'm not sure, but I think there's a town ordinance that requires beach attendance," Sam said, and then laughed.

Obviously Bronwyn didn't get the joke; she kicked at a twig caught in a crack in the sidewalk, scuffing the toes of her dress shoes.

And that was another thing; why, on the last day of school, was the poor kid dressed as though she was having tea with the Queen?

Sam's own grade school days weren't so far in the past that she didn't remember cutoffs or jeans and T-shirts were the preferred attire. The other kids were sure to be wearing casual clothes, and here was Bronwyn in a blue dress with a white pinafore, white ankle socks, and black patent leather shoes.

The uncharitable thoughts about Mrs. Henderson that Sam had banished from her mind returned with a vengeance, along with a few new ones.

"We'll be going to the beach," she said. "As many times as you want."

The kid really had a great smile.

The "walk" signal flashed on, and Bronwyn took her hand as they crossed the street. Another block and they began heading up the slope of the hill on which Bayview Elementary was situated.

A group of kids ran by them, whooping and hollering with the enthusiasm of the soon-to-be-free. One of the boys turned and ran backward, waving at Bronwyn before putting on the gas and speeding past his friends.

Showing off, Samantha knew, remembering with a hint of nostalgia back when it was that easy to tell if a boy liked you. "Who's that?"

"Just a boy."

"A cute boy," she corrected. "Isn't he one of the Cochran kids?"

Bronwyn shrugged at the first and nodded at the

second, but her eyes were looking elsewhere.

They had reached the edge of the school grounds where the swings and slides were located, and it was obvious to Sam what had captured Bronwyn's attention. A girl of her age was on the swings, flying through the air, hair fanned out behind her, her legs pumping as she strove to go higher and higher.

Sam glanced at her watch. The school bell would be ringing in another minute or two, but maybe there was time for a quick swing?

"Do you want to—"

The strident ring of the bell cut her off in midsentence.

Later, she thought.

After delivering Bronwyn safely to her classroom, Sam headed back to the English house.

"Here are the keys," Mrs. Henderson said, dropping a ring which held five keys into her hand. "Don't misplace them. Dr. English has a duplicate set, but it would be very inconvenient for him to have to come home in the middle of the day and let you in."

Sam smiled and nodded. Five more minutes and the taxi would be here to take the housekeeper and her matched luggage to the airport.

"The small one is to the mailbox. The mail comes at three. Leave it here, on the table by the phone." She rested her hand on the gleaming surface of the table as though to remove any doubt; it was the only table in the entryway. "The doctor likes to look at the mail after dinner."

Five more minutes. The smile on her face would need to be surgically removed.

"You can open the mail for him"—Mrs. Henderson held up a silver letter opener—"but use your discretion."

The inflection in the housekeeper's voice suggested that she doubted Sam was capable of being discreet. "I'll try," Sam said.

"Oh, and I've put out Bronwyn's things for her dance class."

Sam followed her into the front room where a small white leather case lay, opened, on the sofa. In it were a pair of pink dance slippers, pink leg warmers, and a black satin leotard.

"There are changing rooms at the studio, and . . . oh-oh, have I forgotten her towel? The class is quite strenuous and she does perspire a bit. . . ."

The words were out before she could stop them. "You actually let her *sweat?*" Sam asked, and then covered her mouth with her hand.

But Mrs. Henderson was already halfway out of the room in search of a towel and apparently hadn't heard her.

Sam slumped down on the arm of the sofa. "Four more minutes," she said aloud. "I can handle anything for four lousy minutes."

Just then a horn honked outside; the taxi had arrived.

Samantha stood on the porch and watched the taxi pull away, her hand raised to wave if the housekeeper looked back. She didn't.

When assured that the taxi wasn't going to pull a U-turn and come back, she went into the house and listened to the blessed silence.

Compared to the challenges of Mabel Henderson's obstacle course of rules, taking care of a quiet eight-year-old would be a piece of cake. . . .

Eleven

Ernie Miller stood at the end of the table, his arms folded across his chest, and watched as his patient struggled to straighten out a bum knee.

The patient, a thirty-three-year-old male, had twisted his left knee playing touch football with a bunch of high-school kids.

Served him right, Ernie thought, making like Bo Jackson minus the talent and a few million bucks. The fool should have known better, should have acted his age, but some people just never learned.

Ernie snapped his gum impatiently. "Come on, you're not trying."

Mr. NFL Running Back glared at him. "I am trying, God damn it."

"Yeah, right." Ernie watched the quadriceps muscle quiver as the guy strained to fully extend the leg. He shook his head. "I've seen white-haired little old ladies work harder than that."

"It hurts," the jock said through clenched teeth.

"No shit. What did you think, you go and twist your knee like a corkscrew, that it wouldn't hurt?" He didn't bother to keep the sarcasm out of his voice; he hated whiners with a passion. "Come on, now.

You want your knee to get better, you've got to take the pain. Be a man about it, pal."

The patient closed his eyes, gripped the edge of the treatment table with both hands, white-knuckling it, and slowly, slowly, straightened his leg.

"Okay," Ernie said, "now hold it, count to ten, you can do it."

Beads of perspiration appeared on the man's forehead and upper lip. ". . . two . . . three . . . four . . ."

"Attaboy."

". . . five . . . it hurts like hell . . . seven . . . eight . . . nine . . . ten."

"Okay, let it down easy, don't drop your leg, there you go. There you go."

The patient opened his eyes and looked at his knee as though he'd never seen it before. He touched the kneecap gingerly. "It feels like someone's jabbing it with a hot poker."

"No kidding? And this is the good part." Ernie held up a hand to ward off the jock's panicked look. "Just a little physical therapy humor. Really, you can get down and soak that sucker in the whirlpool."

"You shouldn't joke about a thing like that." The patient's eyes glinted. "People can take only so much pain . . . and then they start hurting back."

Ernie laughed.

At noon Ernie ushered the last of the morning patients out, locked the department door, got his lunch from his desk drawer, and went into the tiny lounge where Alice, the other therapist, was already eating.

"What a day," he said, collapsing onto the battered Naugahyde couch.

"It's always busy on Friday." Alice took a healthy bite of her apple. Between chews, she said, "They want to be limber so they can party out."

"That's disgusting."

"What is? I *know* you like to party as much as the next guy."

"No. Talking with food in your mouth." He popped the top of his cream soda. "Didn't your mother ever teach you not to talk with your mouth full?"

"Well she might have tried, but I couldn't understand her, 'cause her mouth was always full"—Alice smirked—"and not of food."

"You are so gross sometimes," he said. He'd never gotten used to women talking suggestively, as if they were men or something.

She lifted her shoulders in an elaborate shrug. "I'd rather be gross than be mistaken for Adolph Hitler's evil twin."

"What does that mean?"

"The way you badger the patients." She'd gnawed the apple down to the core, and she tossed it in the general direction of the waste basket. It landed on the floor with a wet plop. "They hate you, you know."

Ernie snorted. "Break my heart."

"I don't know why you have to be that way."

"They get mad," he said, "the adrenaline starts flowing, they push a little harder." He unwrapped his sandwich and lifted the top slice of bread. As usual, the edges of the cheese were dried out. Maybe he ought to pop for those individually wrapped slices.

"Sure," Alice was saying. "And sometimes they push too hard and reinjure themselves."

He glanced up at her. "So? The way I figure, it's job security." He took a bite of the sandwich; it tasted good enough.

"Ha. One of these days you're going to bully the wrong person, and you'll be out on your ass so fast your head will swim."

Ernie finished chewing and swallowed before answering. "And where are they going to find another physical therapist in a town this size? We're it, baby."

"They could recruit—"

"Get real." He pointed at the bulletin board where the "position available" notice from the personnel office was posted. The notice was yellowed with age, the corners curled up, the print faded. "They've been trying to find a third therapist to cover the evening shift for as long as I've been here."

Alice said nothing, only shook her head.

"And for that matter, why'd they hire you? You're supposed to be an occupational therapist, not working in P.T."

"When they get the new hire, I'm going to start doing both."

Ernie laughed. "Dream on. Eighty percent of our work load is providing exercise for the living dead over on West. What kind of occupational therapy did you have in mind for them?"

"Don't call them that—"

"Oh, *I* know. You can train them to be paper-weights. Or maybe there's a need for drooling blobs, and we've got an untapped resource on our hands."

"And you call me disgusting." Alice crumpled up her lunch bag, but this time she got to her feet and walked over to the waste basket to throw it away. "They're human beings, for crying out loud."

"Yeah? Would you want your sister to marry one?"

"You know your problem?"

"I'm sure you'll tell me."

"You're a first-class jerk." With that, she stomped out of the room.

"Hey," he called after her, "what's the point of being a second-class jerk?"

Alice said something indistinguishable—it might have been jackass—and then he heard the outer-office door open and close.

Ernie took a swallow of cream soda and smacked his lips. "What a bitch," he said to no one in particular.

At one-thirty, Ernie showed up on West to give afternoon treatments.

"You're late," the unit secretary said.

"So? It's not like the patients have places to go and things to do. I mean, are they planning on a group ski trip or something?" He laughed at his own wit.

"Very amusing," she said in a voice that indicated otherwise. "Now please get your work done so the nurses can do theirs."

He saluted and would have clicked his heels except that his crepe-soled shoes gripped the floor too well. "At your service."

The secretary raised her eyes heavenward and reached to answer the phone.

Ernie did an about-face and marched down the hall, counting off in cadence. "Your left, your left, your left, right, left . . ."

". . . your left, right, left," he sang under his breath as he flexed and stretched a patient's bony ankle. The ankle was still fairly loose-jointed, but the patient had only been on West for a month and a half. After a dozen or so flexion repetitions, he worked on

97

rotation from side to side, and then in a circular movement.

When he was done with both ankles, he moved up to the knees. Both knees had surfer's knobs on them.

"You should have stuck to surfing," Ernie said, lifting the left leg up off the bed while bringing the heel down until it nearly touched the back of the thigh.

The patient was a sixteen-year-old male who'd lost control of a high-powered motorcycle—or donor cycle, as trauma teams referred to them—he'd borrowed from a friend. Some friend, Ernie thought.

Miraculously, none of the kid's bones had been fractured in the accident, but he had sustained a severe, closed head injury. End result? The kid was now little more than a bag of bones that had to be put through range-of-motion exercises, even though his potential for purposeful motion of any kind was next to nothing.

Ernie sometimes wondered if the best move for any of these coma patients mightn't be pulling the plug.

But the way he looked at it, it wasn't his problem.

He was only the joint jockey.

The last patient on his list was Deborah English.

She had been on West the longest of any of them, some eight years now. The years hadn't been kind to her, although sometimes, in a certain light, from a certain angle, he would look at her and see traces of the beautiful woman she'd once been.

For some reason he'd never quite been able to put a finger on, he found it more difficult to work on her than the others.

There was something about being alone in that room with her that spooked him . . . almost as if he

98

expected to glance up and see her watching him.

The thought sent a shiver up his spine.

Regardless, he had a job to do, and only half an hour before his shift was over. The very last thing he wanted was to be stuck with overtime on a Friday.

With that in mind, he headed resolutely for 6-West.

Twelve

Bronwyn watched the second hand sweep past the six and toward the twelve on the face of the clock. She held her breath in anticipation of the moment she'd been waiting for since September.

Thirty more seconds to summer.

At last.

Around her, her classmates chattered with excitement, totally ignoring Miss Peters who stood at the front of the room after saying her goodbyes. She held one finger to her lips to signal for quiet, but it was too late.

The bell rang.

School was out!

Bronwyn was out of her seat and heading for the door before the bell finished ringing, her arms full of all kinds of papers and drawings and stuff that Miss Peters had handed back. By the door there was a trash can, and she dumped the papers in it and continued on over the threshold without losing a step.

"Bronwyn?" a voice called over the ruckus. "I'm over here."

She turned and spied Samantha at the far end of the hall near the kindergarten classrooms. She ran in

101

that direction, buoyant at the prospect of the long summer days that were ahead of her.

When she got closer, she noticed that Sam was holding her ballet case, and also had a shopping bag from Kandi's, the town's only children's clothes store. Curious, she looked at Sam, who smiled.

"I've got a surprise for you," Sam said. "I bought you a present."

"A present? For me?"

"Absolutely. Wait 'til you see."

Bronwyn allowed herself to be guided into the lower-grade girls' restroom. It was empty—the little kids had gone home at noon—and their footsteps echoed in the small space.

Sam sat on her heels and opened the shopping bag, then pulled out a pair of new but fashionably faded blue jeans and a blue and white checkered short-sleeved blouse. She began removing the price tags and labels.

"I looked in your closet to check out the size," Sam said, holding the blouse up to her, "so these should fit. I was going to get sneakers, too, but the salesman said it would be better if you came in and tried them on. We can do that tomorrow, and I'll also ask your father if I can get some shorts and T-shirts and whatever else we can think of. Here."

Bronwyn accepted the clothes handed to her. "Thank you, but—"

"Go on, change into them."

She fingered the soft denim. "But I have dance class this afternoon."

"At four o'clock. It's only two-thirty; we have loads of time."

"Time for what?"

Sam grinned. "To swing."

* * *

102

The clothes fit perfectly, and Bronwyn luxuriated in the feel of denim against her skin. Walking toward the playground, she pretended to brush something off the pant leg, just so she could touch it, and marvel at the texture of the fabric.

She'd never owned a pair of jeans before.

Mrs. Henderson had instructed her that jeans were one of several items inappropriate for young ladies. "They're altogether too snug in places they shouldn't be," was what she'd said.

Bronwyn hadn't an idea what that meant. But it didn't really matter, since her father had always relied on Mrs. Henderson to take her shopping.

She glanced sideways at the bag from Kandi's, which now held her dress and pinafore, and of course, her slip. Sam hadn't even folded them, just rolled them into a bundle and stuffed them in the bag.

It wasn't hard to imagine what Mrs. Henderson would have said about that.

Sam stopped, putting the shopping bag and ballet case down near the frame of the swing set. "So, kiddo, pick a swing, hop on board, and I'll give you a push to get you started."

Bronwyn did.

She was a little rusty at it—she leaned forward too early in the swing—but before long she was flying through the air under her own power.

She laughed, delighted, as she sailed toward the sky, pausing for a split second of weightlessness before falling back again. The chain clanked and creaked with her efforts, and her hands tightened around the metal links.

A strand of hair blew across her face, tickling her nose until she reversed direction and the wind caught it and pulled it away.

She extended her legs in front of her, and pointed

her toes. Her shiny black shoes looked a little funny with her new jeans but who was there to care? She didn't.

Something moved to the right of her and she saw that Sam had joined her on the swings. Their rhythms were off, she going up when Sam was coming down, but she laughed again at the joy of it, not being alone.

The sun was warm on her face, and her bare arms, and when she felt brave enough, she closed her eyes. Through her eyelids, she saw red.

It seemed to her that time stopped, and all that was left in the world was the sun, the wind, and the clanking of the chains.

She felt breathless with exhilaration.

Bronwyn swung until her hands were sore from holding on, and then reluctantly began to slow.

"Was that fun?" Sam asked.

"I loved it."

"Me too." Sam hooked her arms around the chains and began to twist the swing, digging in with her heels and walking it around. When she'd made five or six circles, she let it unwind, her legs tucked beneath her as she spun. "Try this," she urged.

Bronwyn tried it, spinning with her head tilted back, and enjoyed the slight dizziness that resulted. She reversed direction and did it again.

"You know," Sam said when she'd come to a stop, "I played on these swings when I was your age. My mother would bring me."

"That must have been nice," Bronwyn said. She'd gotten rust from the chains on her hands, and maybe the beginnings of a blister at the base of her right index finger, but she was considering swinging some more.

"It was. I always was eager to get older so I could

come here alone and play, but then"—she smiled sadly—"I got older and I had other things to do."

What other things, Bronwyn wondered, could be better than this?

"I'd forgotten how much fun I had here," Sam said, almost to herself.

"I won't forget." Bronwyn flexed her hand, and decided it really was too tender to grip the chains. Across the play yard she saw the slides.

"Well," Sam said, getting up, "we'd better get going, or you won't be able to 'do a proper warm-up' for your ballet class."

"Can I go down the slide just once?"

Sam looked in that direction. "Can anyone go down a slide just once?"

Bronwyn blinked, not knowing how to answer, but then realized the question wasn't asked of her. Sam was halfway to the slides.

It wasn't really possible to skip across sand or soft dirt or grass, but Bronwyn did the best she could. This was turning out to be a great day.

The cool metal handrails felt good against the chafed skin on her palms as she clambered up the steps of the biggest of three slides. Sam was already at the top, ahead of her, getting into position.

"Here I go," Sam said, then scooted forward, her arms in the air as she made the slide. "Whoa!"

Bronwyn reached the platform, standing on the next-to-last step and watching as Sam zoomed down the slippery surface. Her landing wasn't that great— her legs were long and she kicked up a shower of sand—but she jumped to her feet laughing.

"Come on down," Sam said.

It was trickier at the top than Bronwyn had remembered, mostly because her shoes wanted to slip on the metal, but she held on to one of the handrails and sort of backed onto the platform, intending to turn when she got a chance.

She never got a chance.

Her right foot skated off the platform, pitching her forward. Startled, she tried to grab onto the second handrail, but the raw skin made her hold tentative . . . she felt herself begin to fall.

"Bronwyn!" she heard Sam yell.

Then she hit her head on something, and heard nothing at all.

Thirteen

The physical therapist was still working on Deborah English when Cassie Owens came into 6-West shortly after three P.M., so she spent a few minutes scanning the progress notes in the chart.

The IV she'd started yesterday had infiltrated during the graveyard shift, and had been replaced. The day shift nurse had noted that the nasogastric tube needed to be changed, and had ordered a new tube from Central Supply, but hadn't done the work.

Typical, Cassie thought, leave it for me.

She was considering writing a snide note about the P.M. shift having to do all the scut work when she heard a sharp intake of breath behind her.

"Did you see that?"

Cassie turned. The physical therapist, a wormy kind of guy she hadn't much use for, looked as pale as a ghost. "See what?"

"She moved her hand."

Cassie glanced at Deborah English. The padded arm boards had been removed to allow for therapy, and her hands lay at her sides, the fingers curled slightly. She took a step closer to the bed and looked from one hand to the other. Both were still.

"I don't see anything," Cassie said.

The therapist—Miller—made as though to touch the patient's hand, but then drew back. "I swear to God, I saw her fingers close."

"Were you exercising them?"

"What?"

"Were you exercising her fingers," she repeated slowly, enunciating each word. "Maybe you left her hand closed and only think that you—"

"No." He cut her off, shaking his head emphatically. "I haven't even started on her wrists."

"Did you bump into the bed or something?"

"That wouldn't make her hand close," he said. To prove it, he nudged the bed twice, first gently and then hard. Neither had any effect. "See?"

"Fascinating."

"You don't believe me, do you?"

She sighed. "I don't see that it makes much difference what I believe."

"I didn't imagine it," Miller said. "I'm not hallucinating."

"Well . . ."

"I'm not. She closed her hand, deliberately closed it, and not slowly either. It was fast, like she was grabbing at something."

"That's impossible."

"I know what I saw."

"And I know that *if* she closed her hand, it wasn't a deliberate act. I've seen her EEGs; she isn't capable of conscious thought."

Miller appeared unconvinced.

"Listen," Cassie said, losing patience, "I've got a lot of work to do, so why don't you finish her therapy and get out of my way?"

"I am finished."

That patently wasn't true, but Cassie decided not

108

to challenge him on it. "Fine." She grabbed one of the arm boards and fit it to the patient's arm, securing it with the soft restraints.

He stood for a moment watching, then pivoted and hurried from the room as though he were being pursued by the hounds of hell.

From out in the hall she heard a startled, "Hey!"

Marcia, the lab tech, came into the room, an indignant expression on her face. "What's with him? He almost ran me over."

Cassie shrugged. "I don't know and I don't care. He had some wild notion the patient was grabbing at him or doing some odd thing."

Marcia crossed the room and put her lab tray on the bedside table. "Do you believe him?"

"Let me put it this way; on his best day, the man has only a nodding acquaintance with the truth, and this isn't his best day."

"I hear you."

"Anyway, how hard up would a woman have to be to grab at a lizard like him?"

"She hasn't been laid in eight years," Marcia said.

Cassie made a face. "By my figuring, that'd give her two more years to go without before she'd be desperate enough to settle for him."

Marcia laughed. "Sounds about right."

"Anyway, to paraphrase an old joke, the woman's in a coma, not dead. She can do better."

"Yeah, but can he?" Marcia wrapped a tourniquet above the elbow on the patient's right arm and thumped at the veins, trying to get one to come up.

"I doubt it." Cassie watched as she took the venipuncture needle and sank it cleanly into a vein. With her thumb, she pushed the sample vial into place. Dark blood flowed into the vial.

"Have you taken her temp yet this afternoon? She

feels a little warm."

"No, but I will." Cassie found the electronic thermometer and fitted the stem with a disposable plastic sheath. "I gather her white count is still high."

Marcia nodded as she changed sample vials, palming the full one. "They're thinking pneumonia. Again. That's three times this year."

"So I heard." She positioned the thermometer under the patient's tongue and held it there.

"Did you also hear that Dr. Armstrong is thinking of discontinuing the antibiotic and letting the pneumonia run its course?"

"No."

"Well, he is."

Cassie looked down at her patient's face and tried as hard as she could to feel sorry for her. "What made him change his mind?"

"Who knows?" Marcia removed the tourniquet, covered the puncture site with an alcohol swab and withdrew the needle. She applied pressure on the wound to stop the bleeding. "If they put it to a vote, I don't think there'd be a single no vote from anyone on the staff."

"Oh, there'd be one," Cassie said, thinking of Dr. English. The thermometer beeped that it had a reading, and she took it from Deborah's mouth.

A hundred and three point six. The low-grade fever had made it to the big time; she'd have to call Dr. Armstrong and advise him.

Marcia had lifted the alcohol swab to see if the wound had stopped bleeding. When the lab tech turned away to get a Band-Aid from her tray, Cassie saw the tendons in Deborah's wrist tense and relax.

So Ernie Miller hadn't been imagining things.

Cassie blinked, opened her mouth to tell Marcia, and then thought better of it.

She had no idea what was happening—maybe the fever had somehow triggered nerves that had long been dormant—but she wasn't going to be the one to further delay what had already been put off for far too many years.

If it was true that Armstrong had reached a decision to cancel his order for antibiotics, the patient would probably last another week or so at the most.

Who knew how long this thing would be drawn out if they started trying to determine the cause of the movements she'd witnessed?

Back at the nursing station, Cassie flipped through the Rolodex looking for Dr. Armstrong's private office number. When she found it, she dailed quickly, before she lost her nerve.

The office receptionist put her through to him immediately.

"Dr. Armstrong? This is Owens on West. I thought you should know that Deborah English's temp has spiked to a hundred and three point six."

"Ah . . . that's not good."

"Also," Cassie said, "her IV has been pulled loose."

That elicited a groan. "Not again."

"I'm not sure how it happened, but I think the physical therapist must have done it. I've noticed he's a little vigorous with the exercises on occasion."

"Damn it—"

"I was wondering, Dr. Armstrong," she said with a rush, "if you still want her to have an IV."

111

"Do I what?"

"Do you want to discontinue the IV?" She took a breath and, when he didn't speak, went on, "Her veins are in terrible condition, as bad as any I've ever seen. I doubt that I'll be able to get another line going, and even if I can, it will probably infiltrate as the others have. So maybe it would be best to, uh, stop the IV altogether. Unless you want to come in and do a cutdown?"

There was silence at the other end.

It wasn't easy, but she had to wait him out. She didn't want him to think she was making the decision for him. By suggesting they stop administering intravenous fluids—and by inference, stop the antibiotics—she was in essence asking him to hasten his patient's death.

Make that his patient's inevitable death.

It was a risky move on her part, but if what Marcia said was true and he was actually on the verge of withdrawing certain of Deborah's support systems, then all she was doing was offering him a graceful way to do it.

When a full minute had passed, she heard him clear his throat.

"No," he said, his voice grave, "I don't think I want to do that. No more IVs."

She closed her eyes in relief.

The doctor thanked her, said he'd be in after office hours, and hung up.

Cassie went into 6-West and closed the door. Working quickly, she shut off the IV drip—which, in fact, was running normally—pulled out the needle, and put a dressing over the wound. She threw the tubing in the trash and disposed of the needle in the

112

infectious waste container.

She didn't regret lying to the doctor, and if Miller got in trouble for something he hadn't done, well, tough luck for him.

"You're on your own now," she said to the still form on the bed.

Fourteen

Percy Smitson tapped the pencil's eraser on the edge of the desk as he leafed through the dozen or so specification sheets for the biomedical equipment that would be necessary to open a trauma unit adjacent to the Emergency Room. None of the specs included prices—those were quoted by the sales rep who presumably had to be on hand to revive the faint of heart—but he knew very well that saving lives didn't come cheap.

The question he had trouble with was, was it worth the price? And if so, was it always worth it for everyone, or only sometimes for some people?

Did you save a man in his forties because he still had x number of years of productive life?

Should you let a woman of seventy-odd years die because the insurance companies had established an average life span, and she'd exceeded it?

If the costs of putting back together a nineteen-year-old semiliterate were significantly in excess of his lifetime earning capacity, did you slap on a Band-Aid and walk away?

Could you use a value-to-cost ratio, the way the banks figured mortgage loans? And who would pay the freight for those whose potential could not be measured at the time of service?

The rationing of medical care was a sensitive subject, and it tended to make people emotional. Percy hadn't much faith in emotion as a business guidepost. Or as a personal one, for that matter.

Of course, he couldn't explain any of that to Wyatt English, who was sitting across the desk from him, waiting patiently while he reviewed the specs. Doctors were notoriously willing to bankrupt hospitals in their quest to play God.

"Well?"

Percy closed the file. "I hate to say it, but it doesn't look good. The problem as I see it is that if we somehow could swing a deal and get everything on your wish list, we'd be digging ourselves into a deep financial hole, one we might not get out of."

"I don't believe that—"

"No, hear me out. Say that we upgrade our emergency facilities and increase the staff to handle the most severe trauma cases. Fine. We save a few lives."

"More than a few."

"Possibly. *But,* after we save them, we have no choice but to keep them until they're ready for discharge. That adds a few more in-patients to the census. Maybe we'll need to hire another couple of nurses for the floors, an X-ray tech, and switch one of our per diem lab people to full-time status."

Wyatt English frowned. "None of which is any more than we'd have to do anyway if the census went up due to other causes."

"Granted. But we can't control 'other causes.' We can choose not to overextend ourselves intentionally. The additional cost in salaries alone could put us in a

116

deficit situation within months."

"Increasing our capabilities would also increase billings."

Percy raised his eyebrows; he'd have laid odds that Wyatt wouldn't have given even a passing thought to the billings. "Yes," he conceded, "we'd be billing out at a premium, but we have to take into account that many of the patients will be un- or underinsured."

"I'm not sure I agree with that."

"Unfortunately it's true." Percy leaned back in his chair, steepling his hands on his chest. "The trauma patients we're most likely to see will be primarily victims of automobile or motorcycle accidents. Would you say that's a fair assumption?"

"I suppose."

"All right. Motorcycle accident victims are rather disproportionately young males. Am I right?"

Wyatt nodded slightly.

"Young males have the highest insurance rates for either auto or motorcycle policies, and as a result, they often carry the minimum coverage allowable by law. The standard policy provides only for bodily injury *liability;* it pays the medical costs when you hurt someone else, and not a dime if you hurt yourself."

"Even so—"

Percy held up a hand. "I know what you're going to say. If they don't have adequate coverage—or any coverage—there's good old Medi-Cal. Which pays a tiny portion of the bill and we have to write off the rest."

"That's preferable," Wyatt said quietly, "to writing off somebody's life."

He'd left himself open for that, and hadn't even seen it coming. Damn, what was wrong with him?

117

Why hadn't he phrased it another way? He'd given English the ammunition to shoot him down.

That's preferable to writing off somebody's life.

It was so simple, so succinct, the kind of statement that, if made by a politician, could bring a crowd to their feet.

And he'd fed him the line.

"I think," Wyatt was saying, "we should put this matter before the Board as soon as possible. Arrange a special meeting if necessary."

That wasn't a prospect Percy looked forward to—on the Board there were too many bleeding hearts who braked for whales or some such nonsense—but he could hardly refuse. "All right."

"Good." Wyatt got up to leave. "Call me when you've set it up."

"Sure thing."

He waited until the door was closed and then slammed his fist on the desk. "Damn!"

Things were not going according to plan.

It was essential that the hospital be financially sound, and running smoothly, particularly now, when he was finally within a year or so of attaining his goal.

He'd come to Point Hansen Hospital with one intention: to prove that what had happened in the past was truly past. Yes, he had made some questionable decisions as an assistant administrator at Mercy Hospital. He had overstepped his bounds, exceeded his authority, but with the very best of intentions.

Was it his fault he'd miscalculated the collective mood of the nursing staff? How was he to know that firing one nurse would result in a strike? And that the Registry nurses usually available to substitute for the staff would refuse to cross the picket line? How could anyone anticipate the news media becoming involved?

Worst of all, who knew that the issue—as plastered over the front page of every newspaper in town—would be not the shortcomings of a nurse, but the "reckless endangerment" of patients' lives by a hospital administration which persisted in under-staffing floors.

And that garbage about the "professional integrity" of the nurses . . . talk about coming from out of left field. What did asking them to do a tad more of the paperwork, and make a bed now and then when housekeeping was tied up, have to do with integrity?

He certainly never intended that Mercy would have to transfer patients to other facilities for care. Never in his wildest dreams could he have envisioned a fleet of ambulances ferrying most of the patients away. One had even left by a Medivac helicopter.

A clip of that particular episode had made "film at eleven" on every television newscast in town, along with a few seconds of him hurrying across the parking lot with reporters in hot pursuit.

All he'd done was fire one lousy, impudent nurse. Granted, there was no one immediately available to care for the patients she'd been assigned to, but what was wrong with the other nurses helping out? Were they *that* damned busy in ICU?

He hadn't thought so.

Anyone could make a mistake. His mistake, by being so visible, had exiled him to Hansen's Point. As career moves went, it left something to be desired. Not that he intended to stay.

His rehabilitation as an administrator required that he keep this hospital on the straight and narrow.

Now was not the time to burden it with debt.

It was, he supposed, remotely possible that, if they opened a trauma unit and it proved successful, he might get credit for it, but he was far more interested in escaping blame if it failed.

No, he wasn't inclined to take any chances in that regard. "Better safe than sorry" seemed infinitely more reasonable than "Nothing ventured, nothing gained."

Well, he'd just have to figure out a way to put English off. If he could delay the project for a year, he'd be out of here by the time the ink turned red.

But how to delay it?

"There has to be a way," he said out loud. "There has to be something I can—"

The idea brought him up out of his chair.

A committee.

He said the word with all the reverence it deserved: "Committee."

The beauty of it was that it was so damned simple. He would suggest to the Board that they form a five-member committee to conduct an extensive feasibility study and prepare a report.

That could keep them busy for *months*. Or, if the right people were on it, even—dare he hope?—a year.

"Percy," he whispered, "you are a genius."

The buzzer on his intercom sounded, startling him. He reached across and hit the button. "What is it?"

"Is Dr. English there?"

His secretary must not have been at her desk when English made his triumphant exit. "No, he's not. He left a few minutes ago."

"Do you know where he was going?"

"He didn't say. Why?"

"Emergency is looking for him."

Percy didn't try to hide his irritation. "Well, page him then. That's what the system is for." He hit disconnect before she could ask any more dumb questions.

A moment later, he heard the page: *Dr. English to the Emergency Room, Dr. Wyatt English to the Emergency Room—stat.*

Fifteen

When Samantha heard them paging Dr. English to the Emergency Room she winced.

She had taken responsibility for Bronwyn at two twenty-five P.M.; within thirty minutes, and while under her supervision, the poor kid had fallen off a slide and knocked herself out, if only momentarily.

Fifteen minutes after that, they were in an ambulance on the way to the hospital.

And now, only an hour into her sojourn as caretaker, she was in Emergency, waiting to explain to Wyatt English how his daughter had gotten hurt.

An hour. That, she thought, could very well be the world record in child-care incompetence. Imagine what she might do given a full two months.

"Sam," a voice said.

She looked up to see Dr. English walking toward her. The effort it took to stand to meet him was at the limit of her capacity.

"Dr. English, she's fine," she said hurriedly, to keep him from worrying unnecessarily. "She just got a bump on the head. They're doing X rays."

His eyes searched hers, and then he gave a slight nod. The lines of tension on his face visibly relaxed.

"What happened?"

"Ah." She ran her fingers through the short hair at the nape of her neck. "Well, we were playing on the swings and then Bronwyn wanted to go down the slide and she lost her footing and fell."

"She hit her head?"

"Yes, but the doctor who saw her said it must have been only a glancing blow. She has a tiny cut—the doctor said it wouldn't even need stitches. Here." Sam touched a spot behind her ear as illustration. "It did knock her out for a few seconds."

The concern reappeared in his eyes. "I'd better talk to Frank," he said, and then hurried off.

Sam watched him go through the double doors that led into the treatment area and wished she could follow. Instead she sat down and prepared to wait.

The waiting room is aptly named, she thought; there is nothing else to do *but* wait. Other than a few well-thumbed magazines and an amateurish oil painting of waves crashing on the shore—what else?—there wasn't even anything to distract people from their anxious solitude.

Besides herself, there were four others, two of them apparently were together. She envied them having someone to talk to.

All she had was the voice inside her head. *What must he think of me?*

"I doubt he's thinking of me at all," she said to the voice, and then remembered she wasn't alone.

All eyes were upon her. One of the two who were together nudged the other, and whispered something which caused the second to laugh.

Sam mustered up a weak smile.

Luckily, a nurse came in, crisp and efficient in her white uniform, chart in hand. "Ostowski?" she inquired, and then added, as though the room might

124

be full of Ostowskis, "Adelaide?"

Adelaide Ostowski rose and obediently followed the nurse through the double doors.

Sam managed to catch a peek inside as the doors swung closed after them. Pale yellow curtains provided a measure of privacy in the open ward area, but several of the drapes had been drawn back to reveal empty stretchers.

Neither Wyatt nor Bronwyn was anywhere in sight.

She settled in to wait.

"Have you hurt yourself?" she heard someone ask, and it took her a moment to realize that she was the one being addressed.

A man she hadn't noticed before had taken a seat one away from hers and was staring at her, she thought, somewhat hopefully. "No," she said, "I'm waiting for someone."

"That's not your blood?"

"Not my—" she broke off, and glanced down at her blouse. Sure enough, there were spots of blood spattered all over.

How had she gotten blood on her?

She had run to Bronwyn, falling to her knees beside her, but afraid to as much as touch her in case it would make matters worse. Then, when the child had come around, she'd ordered her not to move, and had dashed off to find a phone and call for help.

After that, she'd returned to the little girl's side, sitting with her and holding her hand, cautioning her all the while to remain still. The ambulance crew had been the ones who'd moved her onto the stretcher.

In the ambulance, she'd sat on a small jump seat

near the door, and had needed both hands to hold on during the ride to the hospital; there'd been no physical contact between her and Bronwyn. And she hadn't even seen Bronwyn since they'd wheeled her through the double doors.

She didn't recall anything she'd done which would explain the presence of blood on her clothes.

The man, who looked as if he hadn't shaved in days and smelled of stale beer, reached with a callused finger as though to touch one of the stains on her blouse. "Maybe you hurt somebody else," he suggested slyly.

She flinched, repulsed by the avid look in his rheumy eyes, and got up quickly, crossing to the reception window. She tapped on the frosted glass with her knuckles and the clerk slid the window open.

"Yes?"

"I'm here with the little girl who was brought in, Dr. English's child, and I was wondering if there's any further word."

"Are you family?"

"No, but I take care of her and I"—she lowered her voice so that no one else would hear—"was the one watching her when she got hurt." Saying it, Sam recognized that she was in essence admitting to what the unshaven man had insinuated she was guilty of.

"I see."

"All I want to know is if she's okay."

The clerk frowned. "Well, let me go and check with a nurse."

"Thank you."

"It'll take a few minutes," the clerk said, and closed the window.

Sam stayed put, preferring to stand rather than return to her seat and risk being accosted again. She sensed that the man was watching her and thought she heard the shuffle of footsteps.

A hand touched her on the shoulder, and she spun, intending to let him have it, only it was Dr. English behind her.

He blinked, apparently in response to the furious expression she hadn't quite blanked from her face. "What's wrong?" he asked.

"Nothing." Over his shoulder, she saw that the man had gone. "I thought you were someone else. How's Bronwyn? Is she okay?"

"She'll be fine. The X rays were normal, nothing's broken."

In her mind's eye she could visualize Bronwyn falling to the ground. She could likewise hear the sound her body had made when she'd landed. It seemed a miracle that she hadn't been seriously injured.

"Thank God," she said. "You've seen her?"

"Yes." He smiled and shook his head. "She wanted me to call her ballet teacher so she wouldn't be marked down for missing a class."

Sam had forgotten all about the infamous dance class. "That reminds me, I think I left her ballet case at the playground."

"Don't worry about it."

"No, I'll go back and get it, if it's still there." He had turned and was walking toward the exit door, and she tagged along.

"There's no hurry."

"But . . . won't she want it?"

"I'm sure she will. However, she's going to have to spend the night here."

"She's being admitted?" Sam touched his arm, making him stop and face her. "I thought you said she was going to be all right."

127

"She is. She might have a slight concussion, and both Frank and I feel it would be best if she remained here for observation. As a matter of fact, they're taking her to her room now. You can come with me to visit her this evening if you want."

Sam had a sinking feeling in her stomach. "Oh, no. I've put her in the hospital."

"Not at all," he said. "Kids are always getting banged up."

"Dr. English, I am so sorry."

"There's nothing to be sorry for." He smiled at her and patted her arm. "And call me Wyatt; I get more than my fill of 'Doctor' every day. Okay?"

Sam was so dumbstruck she just stood there in the middle of the ambulance bay as he walked out, she assumed on his way to his office.

In spite of his assurance that there was no rush, Sam went back to the playground to recover Bronwyn's ballet case before someone made off with it.

It was right where she'd left it, and she kneeled on the grass and opened it to check the contents. Everything seemed to be in order.

Sam touched the thin pink ribbon on one of the small ballet slippers, then took both of the slippers out. Leaving the case on the grass, she walked slowly to the swings and sat down.

The slippers were of satin, she supposed, and looked fairly new. These weren't the toe slippers ballerinas used to dance on point; Bronwyn was much too young for that. These were soft and supple, and almost unbearably small.

To think that in her eagerness to make friends with a little girl she might have brought about serious

128

injury. A fall such as that could have broken arms or legs or even the child's neck.

It might have left her paralyzed, or worse.

Sam held the pink slippers in both hands, one thumb stroking the satin, and lowered her head. She stayed there, swinging gently, until the bad feelings passed.

Sixteen

"Is she all right then?" Eva Quintero asked when Wyatt returned to the office.

"Bronwyn's fine. She's got a bump on the head and a quarter-inch laceration that was closed with steristrips. And she's being very brave about having to stay in the hospital overnight.

"Of course she's brave, and why wouldn't she be? It isn't a scary place to her the way it is to most children. I'll bet she knows her way around those halls as well as you do."

Wyatt took his lab coat from the hook and slipped it on. "You may be right."

"Even so, I think I'll send her a little bouquet of flowers or a stuffed animal."

"You'll spoil her, Eva."

"Never," she scoffed, sitting at her desk and reaching for the Rolodex. "She's too much her father's daughter for that to ever happen."

"Meaning?"

"It means she's a perfectly sweet child who appreciates any nice thing you do for her; a spoiled child is one who comes to take nice things for granted, as being her due."

He smiled. Coming from Eva, it was high praise. "She is a nice kid, isn't she?"

"You're darned right."

If anyone knew about nice kids, it was Eva; her own three children—she'd raised them alone after the death of her husband from a heart attack in 1980— had turned out great. The eldest, Sarah, was in her last year of medical school; the middle child, Timothy, was at the top of his class at Annapolis; and Ruth Ann, the baby, had just graduated from high school as valedictorian.

"Now," she said, feigning exasperation, "get to work or we'll be here 'til midnight seeing patients."

"Yes, ma'am," he said.

The rest of the afternoon went relatively well. None of Wyatt's patients were terribly sick. Most were in with the usual complaints—summer colds, mild cases of the flu, allergies, and assorted aches and pains attributable to either arthritis or just plain overdoing it—and he was able to maintain an even pace.

Betty Cochran brought her son Jason in for a sports physical, along with a batch of homemade double-fudge brownies.

"You could use a little weight," Betty said, eyeing him speculatively. "With Mabel gone all summer, you might up and waste away on us."

Wyatt inserted the tip of the otoscope into Jason's left ear and peered through. "I doubt that." The tympanic membrance was patent, and there were no signs of inflammation, which was good. If the Cochran boys had a weakness, it was their ears.

"What are you going to do about meals then?"

"Eat them, what else?" He turned Jason's head to

check the right ear.

"No, I mean, well . . . Samantha Townsend is a lovely girl and I'm sure she'll be wonderful with Bronwyn, but can she cook?"

It was such an unexpected question that he laughed. "I don't know, Betty, I never asked her."

"Honestly! *Men.*"

The right ear looked normal, and he withdrew the otoscope. "Doing great, champ," he said, and mussed Jason's straw-colored hair.

"I'd be glad to have you and Bronwyn over to dinner sometime," Betty said. "Jason would like that, too, wouldn't you, Jason?"

Jason turned a dusky shade of red and glared at his mother. "Mom," he said, dragging a one-syllable word out to sentence length.

"That's very kind of you." Wyatt reached for a tongue blade, and cupped his hand beneath the boy's chin, tilting his face up. "Open wide."

"It's nothing more than any good neighbor would do. So, shall we plan on it?"

"Say 'ah,'" he instructed, placing the wooden blade near the base of the boy's tongue.

Jason complied.

His throat looked fine. "That'll do it," Wyatt said. He discarded the blade and stripped off his latex gloves. He turned to Betty Cochran. "I don't know about dinner; let me ask Sam what would be convenient for her."

Betty's eyes widened. "Oh, well, of course, she's invited too, if she wants to come, but I thought, well, she's young and maybe she'd appreciate having a night off. You and Bronwyn could have a nice quiet evening with us and she could go out with her friends, which she'd probably enjoy more anyway."

"I hadn't thought of that," Wyatt admitted. Mabel

was an avowed homebody, content to spend her evenings with Bronwyn; he couldn't recall the last time she'd gone out socially at night.

"So . . . it's settled. How's Tuesday look?"

"I can't promise right now, but we'll see." He seldom cared to be evasive, but he wasn't sure how Bronwyn would be feeling in the next few days. Under normal circumstances, he'd tell Betty as much, but he'd decided earlier against mentioning his daughter's accident to any of his patients. He was, quite frankly, somewhat weary of his family being an object of concern.

And in any case, he wanted to ask Sam if she'd like to join them.

Betty, however, looked pleased. "Good. Call me, and if Tuesday's bad, we'll make it another day."

The rest of the exam passed uneventfully. He filled out the form, attesting that Jason Cochran was physically sound enough to play baseball for the summer league, and then followed the boy and his mother out of the examining room to the front desk.

"Would you make a copy of this for the chart?" he asked Eva, handing her the form.

"Right away."

"Oh, and, Wyatt," Betty Cochran said, "be sure to let me know if there's anything Bronwyn doesn't care to eat. I know how finicky kids can be. . . ."

Eva came back with the form and a photocopy, handed the original to Mrs. Cochran without comment, then interrogated Wyatt with her eyes as the Cochrans left.

"Well?" she said, hands on her hips.

He made one last note on the chart and handed it to her. "Well what?"

"Why does Betty Cochran look like the cat that got the canary?"

134

"Did she?"

"She certainly did."

"I'll be damned if I know."

"Hmm. And what was that business about what Bronwyn doesn't like? She isn't planning on taking the child food when she's in the hospital, is she?"

"No. She's invited us to dinner."

Eva's eyebrows arched. "Oh, really."

Wyatt knew Eva well enough to detect the disapproval behind her response. "What's wrong with that?"

"Did you know that Harvey Cochran moved out of their house last month?"

"I hadn't heard."

"He's taken up with a drum majorette who used to date the oldest boy, if you can believe that. But Betty isn't the type to take it lying down, and"—Eva reached out and plucked the sleeve of his lab coat—"what's this? A feather?"

There was nothing in her fingers and he shook his head, not understanding.

"I do believe she thinks you're the canary who could even the score."

"I'm not interested in being anyone's canary," he said, and went on to the next patient.

At six, he finished with the last patient of the day and went to his private office to make a few calls. He heard Eva talking with someone, but thought nothing of it.

He was listening to a line ring when someone tapped on his door. He swiveled in his chair so that he was facing the door, and his heart rate quickened.

Eva stood in the doorway, and behind her, looking grim, was Tony Armstrong, Deborah's doctor.

Wyatt sat forward and slipped the phone receiver into the cradle.

"Wyatt," Armstrong said, "I need to talk to you."

All he could think of was that Deborah had died, and Armstrong had come to tell him in person. He closed his eyes briefly before getting to his feet and extending his hand across the desk.

Dr. Armstrong's grip was firm as they shook hands. Eva left, closing the door after her.

"I'll get right to it," Armstrong said, but then hesitated. He rubbed the bridge of his nose between thumb and forefinger, and sighed.

Wyatt forced himself to wait.

"This is difficult for me, but I wanted you to hear it from me. . . . I feel that the time has come for us . . . for you . . . to let Deborah go."

Then she's still alive.

"It's probable that she's developing pneumonia again. Her temperature is over a hundred and three—"

"She isn't responding to the antibiotics?"

"That's the problem." Armstrong's eyes evaded his. "I've decided to discontinue the antibiotics. We've been having a hell of a time keeping an IV going. Even if we could, her kidneys aren't tolerating the medication, and it's likely that the buildup in her blood could prove toxic."

"I see."

Armstrong sighed again. "What I'm saying is, it doesn't look good."

"But she's been through this kind of thing before. Try a different drug, or give it intramuscularly."

"Wyatt, I can't do it." He leaned forward, his voice urgent. "Let her go. Don't put her—or yourself—through any more."

"You don't know what you're asking me to do,"

136

Wyatt said.

"Yes I do. And I know it won't be easy for you. But it is the right thing to do, I'm sure of that." Armstrong frowned. "I don't think either of us wants to see her last hours be as hard as they might be if we continue the way we've been going."

Wyatt was silent.

"Last night I was on West when a patient arrested. We worked for the better part of an hour trying to bring him back. We broke his ribs doing CPR—"

"I've run codes, Tony. I know all about broken ribs."

"But don't you see?" Armstrong got up and paced, gesturing with both hands. "If we don't back off, it will be Deborah. *Deborah.*"

Wyatt didn't want to think of that, but found it impossible not to. The familiar sights and sounds of reviving a patient in full cardiac arrest filled his mind, relentless in their clarity.

There was a brutality about it, the patient laid bare and becoming, for the duration of resuscitation, little more than a body, curiously without an identity.

Wyatt shook his head to clear it of those thoughts. To him, Deborah was always the way she'd been when he'd first met her, and he carried that image of her with him.

"Let her go," Armstrong repeated. "She deserves a gentle end."

"But what if—"

"There are no 'ifs' left."

And Wyatt finally knew that was true. "All right," he said. "Do what you feel is best for her."

Seventeen

Eva Quintero left the office by the side door, locking it behind her, and headed for her car in the small parking lot. The other offices in the complex were long since closed; there were only three cars in the lot: her Honda, Dr. English's Jaguar XJ6, and, she supposed, Dr. Armstrong's Mercedes-Benz.

Ordinarily when she worked overtime she waited for Dr. English to walk her out, because it was often dark by the time they finished. But thanks to daylight savings time it was still light although it was nearly seven o'clock.

Even if it had been dark, Eva thought she wouldn't have waited on this night, though.

She wondered what Dr. Armstrong had come to say.

There had been a fleeting moment when she'd considered trying to listen to the conversation, but her self-esteem wouldn't allow that. She didn't care ever to be the type of person—a Mrs. Goldstein—who would press her ear against a door.

Anyway, whatever was going on wasn't any business of hers. If Dr. English wanted to tell her, he would. If he didn't, he wouldn't.

Eva buckled her seat belt and turned the key in the ignition, then noticed that the gas gauge read empty. Ruth Ann had borrowed the car last night to go to a show with her friends.

"Darn kid," she said.

She pulled into the self-service island at the gas station and got out to pump her own gas.

"Can I do that for you, Mrs. Quintero?"

Eva turned and recognized the attendant as Bobby Cochran. After having Betty and Jason in the office that day, it seemed to her there were Cochrans everywhere she looked.

Bobby had bulked up since she'd last seen him and now appeared slightly menacing, even with the trademark Cochran smile. "I suppose you could, but don't expect me to pay full service prices. I can't afford it."

"No problem." He grinned and took the nozzle from her, removed the gas cap from the tank, and jammed the spout in. Somehow he balanced it so it stayed put without him holding it.

The digital dial on the gas pump registered the cost at an alarming rate, the numbers flickering as they changed. Eva began digging in her purse, to see if she had enough to fill the tank or needed to stop at ten dollars' worth, and realized that in all the excitement of Bronwyn's accident, she'd forgotten to remind Dr. English to sign her paycheck, which she'd left on his desk.

She wouldn't make it through the weekend without that check; she'd have to go back to the office. "You idiot," she said in disgust.

"Excuse me?"

The young man looked offended. "I'm sorry, Bobby, I was talking to myself. Only ten dollars' worth, please."

"It's already past that—"

"Then stop or you'll have to siphon it out."

He did as he was told: "It's eleven dollars and sixty-eight cents, but you can owe me if you don't have the money handy."

"No, I've got it, but just." She gave him the ten she kept folded and tucked away beneath Timothy's baby picture, a one-dollar bill that had been put through the wash, and counted out sixty-eight cents in change, most of it nickels and pennies.

Bobby waited patiently, his mouth moving in a silent echo of her accounting.

"There," she said.

"Thank you." His big hand closed around the cash. "Pardon me for asking, Mrs. Quintero, but doesn't Dr. English make a lot of money?"

She squinted at him, annoyed. "What kind of question is that?"

"Well, he must not pay a good salary if you are, you know, short of funds, because I'm working here, at minimum wage, you know, and I've got money in my pocket, but you haven't. And I was wondering, you know, what kind of living he makes."

It took her a second to reconstruct what he'd said into what she could understand, and when she did, she didn't like it. "Why? Are you planning to go to medical school?" she asked archly.

"Me?" He laughed. "No way. But my mother is always saying how rich he is. That's all she talks about these days, and—"

"Your mother." The woman and her infernal double-fudge brownies. So that really *was* what Betty Cochran was up to, thinking she'd snag a wealthy husband, since hers had gotten away.

"—he drives that nice car, which I know has to go for at least fifty grand, so I figured—"

Eva held up a hand. "Never mind. For your information, I am paid quite well, but I *do* have a daughter in medical school, and another about to start college, and education is expensive, but of course neither you nor your mother would know that." If the entire family got together and rubbed their collective brain cells together, it wouldn't create enough heat to roast a marshmallow.

There was an expression of bewilderment on Bobby's face. "Huh?"

"Forget it. It's not you I'm mad at." She got into the car and closed the door gently—she was embarrassed at having vented her anger on poor Bobby who in any battle of wits would have to be considered unarmed—and drove out of the station.

Eva was greatly relieved to see that Dr. English's car was still in the lot, and she pulled in beside it. The Mercedes was gone.

She hurried to the side door, her key in hand, anxious about the growing approach of darkness. Sometimes, as silly as it was, she couldn't shake the feeling that she was being watched.

The door opened as she reached it.

"Dr. English," she said, somewhat breathlessly, "I went off and forgot my check."

He looked at her strangely, uncomprehendingly, as if he were from another country and didn't speak the language.

"What is it?"

He said nothing at first, shaking his head, while the muscles in his throat moved and his jaw clenched. Then his eyes met hers. "Deborah."

Just that, the one word.

"Is she . . . ?"

142

"No."

Eva had never seen him this way in all the years she'd worked for him, but if his wife hadn't died, what could it be that was tearing him up?

"Come back inside," she said, "and tell me."

He allowed her to usher him through the door and into the hall where he stood, leaning against the wall, as she locked them in.

There was almost no light in the hall, only that which filtered through the venetian blinds, and it was rapidly fading, but she sensed that it might be easier for him to talk if she couldn't see his face.

And easier for her as well.

She hung her purse on the doorknob and went to stand at his side. "Wyatt?" She almost never called him that, but it felt right to her now. "Dr. Armstrong had bad news about Deborah?"

"We're going to let her die."

His voice was a whisper, and the sound of it sent a shiver through her. She of course had never met Deborah, and had seen her only twice, once that first year, and then this past fall, but she had come to feel she knew her, as Bronwyn's mother and Wyatt's wife.

Though there were times when she thought it would be best for both of them if Deborah had died, there were also times when she wished to spare them that final pain, forever if it were possible.

Now she didn't know what to say. She took his hand and squeezed it.

"I told him, all right." He rested his head on the wall.

"Told Dr. Armstrong?"

"Yes."

She wasn't sure she understood, but it didn't matter. He needed to talk; she would listen.

"It won't be long," he said. "A week or two."

143

Perhaps it was her imagination, but she felt as if the darkness had deepened all of a sudden. It was an oddly disorienting thing, standing in the dark. She found that she had to place her free hand on the wall to keep from losing her balance.

Wyatt had lapsed into silence again.

An indeterminate amount of time passed. His hand was now holding hers tightly, and he had brought it up to his face.

She thought of Ruth Ann, home and awaiting dinner, but as the youngest child, Ruth Ann had learned to fend for herself. In any case, this was where she was needed the most right now.

"What do I do?"

The question caught her off-guard, but she answered anyway. "You go on. When Deborah dies, you mourn her, and then you go on with your life." This she knew from experience, so she continued: "It will be hard at first, very hard, and you'll wonder if you can get through a day without missing her, but the time will come when the hurt is nearly gone."

"Will it?"

The haunted quality of his voice brought back with such force the despair she'd endured at her husband's passing that she nearly wept, but she needed to be strong for him. It took a moment to regain her composure.

"I know right now you don't believe it," she said, "but you will get over this. I promise."

He brought her hand to his lips and kissed it, and she felt the wetness of his tears. Her heart ached for him, and the long, lonely nights to come.

"You'll be okay," she soothed, "both of you."

"I have to tell Bronwyn," he said. "I have to prepare her."

"I think she knows," Eva said.

144

Eighteen

Bronwyn took a sip of fruit juice as she studied the tic-tac-toe game board. She was playing X and Sam was O, and of the dozen or so games they'd played, she had won all but one.

"This year, please," Sam said.

"I'm thinking." Bronwyn poised the pencil over the upper right outside box, and then hesitated. She chewed on the eraser while she considered her options.

Sam, who was sitting on the bed beside her, gave her a gentle nudge. "Well, think faster. I have a life, you know, kid."

"Not playing *this* game."

"You little snip," Sam said, and laughed. "Show some respect for your elders."

Bronwyn fought back a smile, unsuccessfully, as she made an X in a square.

As soon as she'd done so, Sam took the pencil from her hand, made a quick O, and said, "Your reign of terror is at an end."

"You think." The younger girl retrieved the pencil and with elaborate care made her final X and then drew a line diagonally through the winning row.

"I win."

"Ouch. That's it, I give up." Sam slipped off the bed and stood, arching her back as she stretched and yawned. "Anyway, it's getting late, and visiting hours were over a long time ago."

"You can stay," Bronwyn said. She knew that the nurses were being extra nice because her father was a doctor. So far they'd brought her two vanilla ice-cream cups and a grape Popsicle.

"Well . . . until your dad gets back."

"Good."

Sam wandered over to the window. "It's so light out, tonight must be the full moon. Boy, it sure is pretty, big and orange-colored."

Bronwyn knew that kind of moon. She wanted to get up and look, but if the nurses caught her out of bed again, they wouldn't be too happy. So she closed her eyes and remembered. The pillows that cushioned her were awfully cozy. . . .

Her father's voice said, "Is she asleep?"

"Playing possum, I think."

Bronwyn peeked from under her eyelashes at them, and then grinned, sitting up and holding out her arms to him. "Hi, Daddy."

Her father came to her side and leaned over to give her a kiss. "How are you feeling?"

She touched her fingers to the small dressing on her temple. "My head aches."

"A funny thing about human anatomy; if you fall and land on your head, it's going to ache," he said. "How about your neck? Is it stiff?"

"The *doctor* already asked me that."

Her father raised his eyebrows. "Oh, that's right. I'm only your father, not your doctor. I forgot all about patient-doctor confidentiality."

"I didn't," his daughter said.

"She's been that way ever since *I* got here," Sam said. "You'd never think so with that sweet face of hers, but she's a sassy little thing."

Bronwyn giggled. "I am not."

"Are too."

"Am not."

Her father held his hands up. "All right, you two. I can see I'm not going to get a straight answer tonight. And even if I'm not your doctor, young lady"—he looked directly at her—"you need to get some rest, and that's father's orders."

"I'm not even tired," she protested.

"You're never tired. Regardless, it's late, and you're going to sleep, now."

"But, Daddy—"

"Good night, Bronwyn." He reached over and turned off the lamp.

The room grew only slightly darker; the door was open, letting in light from the hall. Better yet, the curtains hadn't been drawn and the sky outside was aglow with moonlight.

Her father kissed her again, and stroked her hair. "We'll be in first thing in the morning to see you, and Sam will take you home."

Sam had come up on the other side of the bed, and she held Bronwyn's hand for a few seconds. "And I'll find a game I can beat you at."

Bronwyn watched them walk out together, and heard their footsteps as they went down the hall. She also heard her father say something, and Sam reply, but she couldn't make out the words.

When their voices faded, she was alone.

The hospital was settling down, with only the faraway sound of ringing phones and an occasional whispered exchange as the nurses passed each other in the hall to break the quiet.

Bronwyn pulled the covers up to her neck and wished that she was home in her own bed. These sheets weren't as soft as hers, and they smelled strongly of bleach. The extra pillows were nice, but she'd rather have her teddy bear, Homer, to snuggle with.

This was the first time in her life she'd ever spent a night away from home.

Some of the other girls in her class had sleepovers, or pajama parties, but even though she was usually invited, she'd never gone to one. Partly because Mrs. Henderson took "a dim view of such goings-on," and partly because Bronwyn didn't really want to go, since she suspected it was the mothers—and not the girls—who'd thought to ask her in the first place.

She hadn't any close friends among girls her age, either at school or at dance class. At dance class there often wasn't time to talk, and even when there was, she found she was uncomfortable talking to girls whose eyes were always seeking their own reflections in the mirrors which lined the walls.

The girls at school weren't any better; they formed groups of three or four, and anyone who wasn't in their group was treated as an outsider. They made jokes only they understood, and passed notes, and turned quiet if you walked past them.

In December, a new girl, Lisa, had joined her class and had been assigned to the desk next to hers. Bronwyn thought they might become friends, but then one of the other girls discovered that Lisa lived on her street, and after that, Lisa went off with them.

Bronwyn guessed maybe Kenny was her friend, sort of. He ate lunch with her, she knew, because the other boys teased him and made fun of him.

And there was Jason, who liked her for reasons she didn't know.

And now there was Sam. Sam of the swings and slides and games. Sam who had promised to take her to the beach and had hinted there were other fun things in store for her this summer.

Bronwyn smiled, and turned to lie on her side, drawing the sheet up so that it covered her face at an angle, with only her eyes showing. The sheet captured her breath as she exhaled, and warmed her.

Eventually, she fell asleep.

A dream?

Bronwyn dreamt that her eyes were open and a shape was hovering near her bed.

Her body tingled, a shivery feeling, and feld cold, dreadfully cold. Something icy touched her face, causing it to go numb.

Bronwyn.

Her name seemed to echo in her head, and in her dream she covered her ears with her hands so that she wouldn't hear the terrible rasping voice that had called her. But then she heard it again:

Bronwyn.

She whimpered, frightened, wanting the dream to be over, the cold feeling to go away.

Look at me.

She resisted, closing her eyes as tightly as she could and pulling the sheet over her head. She burrowed deeper in the bed.

You are my child.

With every ounce of will in her, Bronwyn tried to come awake. Twice she pinched her own arm, hard, and felt the pain, but the horrible feeling in the pit of her stomach remained and the dream went on.

Come to me.

She opened her mouth to cry out, but at that instant, what felt like a sliver of ice entered her right eye, its coldness burning into her brain. The scream died in her throat from a lack of air.

You are my child.

The chill spread through her, encompassing her in a frigid shroud. Her body had begun to shake uncontrollably, and she could feel her teeth chattering. She bit her tongue and tasted blood.

Bronwyn, the voice whispered, *I have been waiting for you.*

Something very much like fingers stroked her hair as her father had done earlier, and then she felt a kiss on her frozen cheek.

Unable to awake from the dream, she escaped into unconsciousness.

"There, there, you'll be all right. You've had a bad dream."

She opened her eyes cautiously. A nurse was at her bedside, gathering up the sheet and blanket to cover her.

"I'm so cold," she said.

"You'll be warm in a few minutes," the nurse promised, and tucked the blankets around her.

"So cold."

"Shh. Go back to sleep."

Her eyelids were so heavy that she could not keep them open. With her eyes closed, it seemed as though the room were revolving around her.

"Cold," she said, and licked her dry lips. They tasted of the blood from her dream.

"Sleep now," the nurse said. "Everything's fine."

Saturday

Nineteen

June 16th

The thing that Gordon hated most about working the graveyard shift at Point Hansen Hospital was eating dinner at two-thirty or three in the A.M. There was something unnatural about biting into a meatball sandwich in the middle of the night when most people were sound asleep in their beds.

Sometimes, too, when he warmed up his dinner in the microwave in the employee lounge, the smell of the food got to him, and he would have to chew a half-dozen Rolaids to keep from tossing his cookies. This being the exact same food whose aroma would leave him drooling at any other time of day.

But what the hell, they were paying a nice, what they called, shift differential for him to work nights. The way he figured, an extra fifteen percent in the old paycheck bought a lot of antacid.

Now, standing in front of the microwave, watching his sandwich get nuked, he waited to see if this was going to be a good night or a bad one. So far, he couldn't smell a thing, even though he could see the mozzarella begin to bubble.

Gordon always held his hand over where he judged his heart to be when he used the microwave; there was a sign on the wall above it, warning people with pacemakers not to use it. He didn't have a pacemaker, but his mamma, rest her soul, had been purely convinced that anything that could cause an egg to blow up with enough force to crack the custard cup it was being cooked in might do the same to the human heart.

His eyes shifted from his sandwich to the timer, which was working down to less than a minute. The faint scent of meat and cheese wafted to his nostrils.

The moment of truth.

He felt the saliva begin to collect in his mouth, but it could go either way. Hunger or nausea, which would it be? Was it . . . was it . . . it was hunger.

"Thank you," he said with a fervent glance heavenward, and drew the smell in deeply.

The microwave dinged that his sandwich was ready just as the lights above him flickered. Another power outage? They'd had one last month. Luckily, the hospital had a backup generator.

But though the lights dimmed almost to the point of extinction, they did not go out.

That's good, he thought, carrying his dinner over to the small round table where his Diet Coke waited. He had a shit-load of floors to be waxing and polishing tonight—the entire west wing—and he didn't need any downtime to get him behind before he even started.

Gordon put the paper plate down, flipped the chair around so it was backward, and sat down to eat.

The night-shift nurses on West were laughing about something when he came up to the station

154

pushing his Handy Dandy floor-waxing machine.

"Gordon," one of them said, "help settle an argument. Do you think Percy wears silk panties under those three-piece suits of his?"

"I wouldn't be surprised." Gordon leaned his elbows on the counter and grinned at them. "It'd sure help explain why the man is so damned prissy."

"What do you think, then? White with little red hearts on them?"

"No, no," a second nurse said. "Redheads are partial to black lingerie."

The secretary shook her head. "You're both wrong. The man has hot pink written all over him."

Gordon considered all possibilities, then said, "I kind of see him in something a little more subtle. Maybe peach with a fancy lace trim . . . and a bull's eye on his backside, so all of us will know where to kiss his ass."

They burst into laughter, which rang in the otherwise silent halls. For a couple of minutes at least, they laughed, and every time it seemed as though they'd get control of themselves, one of them would make loud kissing sounds, and that'd set the others off.

"Please," the first nurse said, "stop. My sides are aching."

"She's right," the secretary announced, pulling a straight face from out of thin air. "We must show a little decorum. After all, this *is* a hospital."

"Oh God, that's right; it is." The second nurse lowered her voice to a whisper. "We wouldn't want to wake the patients."

Gordon snorted. "Honey, you could tap-dance across their chests and not wake these patients."

"The hell with it then," she responded, and then let out a warbling whoop that would have done old vine-swinging Tarzan proud.

And that was the end of their decorum.

Gordon guided the waxer in wide, semicircular sweeps, still chuckling to himself.

If eating at night was the worst of this job, the people who worked graveyard were the best of it. The night nurses weren't snobs like the gals on day shift, who thought they were above associating with a janitor, or, as they called him nowadays, a maintenance engineer.

These nurses were down-to-earth, friendly, outgoing, and not afraid to speak their minds. The word that best described them—he'd looked it up in the dictionary—was irreverent.

What he wasn't sure about was whether they were working the graveyard shift because they were irreverent *or* they were irreverent because they were working graveyard. That kind of chicken-or-egg, which-came-first question always threw him for a loop.

He did know the day and evening shifts were locked into hospital politics, and that wasn't good for anybody as far as he could see. It got to the point where the day shift was absolutely certain they were doing the majority of the work and the other two shifts were goofing off. Of course, P.M.'s thought the exact same thing about the day shift and graveyard.

Graveyard, bless them, knew they didn't pull as heavy a load, and didn't really give a fig who knew it. The graveyard point of view was that giving up sleeping at night pretty much evened the score.

Of course, in his own department, things were simpler. Floors didn't know what time of day it was, and assignments were figured in square yards.

As for him, specifically, he often was assigned the office areas and the west wing. The offices because it was the only time when there weren't people around to get in the way, and West because there no amount of noise would wake these patients up.

"Tap-dance across their chests," he reminded himself, and laughed again, ending with a sigh.

He flicked on the lights to 6-West, and maneuvered the waxer through the doorway.

"I won't be but just a minute, darling," he said to the woman in the bed. It was his habit to talk to them; he liked to be sociable.

There were all kinds of electrical cords under and about the bed, and he began to reel them in, winding each in turn around his right hand and then placing the coiled cord on top of its machine.

Gordon whistled softly as he worked, the sound barely audible over the hiss of the ventilator. He had to make up for time lost jawing with the nurses.

He had gathered all of the power cords but one when the lights dimmed again. He looked at the fluorescents overhead, waiting to see what would happen.

Nothing did, although when the lights came up, it seemed that they weren't quite as bright as before. Possibly, he thought, a bulb going bad. He would make a note to remind himself to bring one from the store tomorrow night.

Gordon finished with the last cord, placing it on a monitor. The image on the monitor screen traced the beating of the patient's heart. He was no doctor, but he'd seen enough of the tracings to be able to tell that this heart was going fast.

Very fast.

For a moment he hesitated, wondering if he should call a nurse to take a look. But didn't they have alarms at the desk for that purpose? He thought they did.

He took a step closer to the bed and studied the face of the patient for any signs that she was in trouble. In the hollow of her throat, her pulse beat rapidly, until it was almost a flutter.

Had her eyes been partially open when he'd come into the room?

"Jesus," he said.

He looked around for the call button. Usually it was safety-pinned to the sheet by the pillow, so the patient could reach it easily, but there wasn't a need for that on West.

There wasn't a phone, either.

The heart rhythm quickened still, and without thinking, Gordon reached with both hands to grab the monitor, as if he could shake it and make it stop.

It was like grabbing hold of a high-voltage cable; a charge of electricity coursed through him, blackening his skin where he touched the monitor, and fracturing all of the small bones in his hands.

He had time enough to smell his own flesh cooking, and nothing more.

Twenty

Percy Smitson parked his car straddling the line, and had the door opened before it came to a full stop. He got out and started for the hospital, realized he'd left his headlights on, and had to go back.

He wasn't used to driving in the pitch-black, early morning hours.

After turning off his lights, he hurried across the parking lot, skipping a few steps as he tucked a finger into his shoe to slip his heel in all the way. The leather rubbed at the tender bare skin; he hadn't had time to put on socks. His feet were perspiring already.

The mercury-vapor lamps cast an eerie glow across the hospital grounds. The buildings hugged the dark landscape, with only an occasional window fully illuminated to reveal there was life within.

It almost didn't look like his hospital.

He went in through Emergency—the only un-locked entrance—and noticed the security guard talking with the duty nurse. He glared at them both.

"Are the police here?"

"Not yet." The nurse straightened, adjusting her too-tight uniform over ample hips. "The body is still

159

on West."

"*Don't* say that."

"Dr. Rojas is also there."

Rojas was one of the Emergency physicians, a quietly capable young doctor considered to be one of their best. "He couldn't do anything for . . . for him?"

"The man was dead in seconds," the nurse said bluntly. "No one could have saved him."

The security guard, who'd been listening in silence, cleared his throat. "It's not a pleasant sight, Mr. Smitson, but if you want to see for yourself, I'll walk over there with you."

Percy waved an impatient hand. "I know the way."

He was relieved that he had arrived in advance of the police, who were sure to complicate matters.

If it had been up to him—and it should have been—he'd have put off calling the police until he had a clear idea of what had happened. Unfortunately, the nursing supervisor had jumped the gun, so to speak, and had called him only after she'd already reported the death to the authorities.

He turned the corner and started down the hall to West, his eyes focused on the double doors that separated the wing from the rest of the hospital. Oddly, he felt as if he were entering unknown territory, even though he'd walked this hall hundreds of times before.

When he reached the doors, he stopped and took a breath, squaring his shoulders in preparation for taking charge. When he was ready, he went through.

The first person he saw was the unit secretary. She was sitting on the desk, leaning forward, her hands entwined and resting on her knees. Her dark hair was swept forward, shielding her face from view.

"Where is Dr. Rojas?" Percy asked, and was pleased to note that she jumped a bit.

Whether from the lateness of the hour or the shock she'd been through, she seemed slow to comprehend what he'd asked. "Dr. Rojas?"

"Dr. Rojas. Where is he?"

"He's with . . . he's in room six."

"Six?" That was Wyatt English's wife's room.

The secretary nodded.

Percy glanced in that direction. Light streamed from the doorway, but otherwise there were no outward indications that something had gone wrong inside. "Very well," he said. "When the police show up, ask them to wait here and come to get me."

She looked at him without expression.

"Do you understand? Come and get me."

"I've got it."

He thought he detected a hint of insolence in her manner, but this wasn't the time or place to deal with it. So he settled for giving her a stern look, one that he'd practiced in front of a mirror.

She surprised him; a corner of her mouth twitched, as though she was fighting a smile.

Disconcerted, he stomped down the hall, but tempered his stride a bit when his toes began sliding around inside his shoes. He actually heard a kind of wet, squishing noise as he walked.

Midway to 6-West, he caught a whiff of a peculiarly sweet odor.

What on earth was *that?*

The first person he saw was Dr. Rojas, whose expression was that of someone who has witnessed too much, an uneven mix of resignation and indignation.

"Percy," Dr. Rojas said. "We have a mess here."

161

He looked where Rojas indicated. The body lay on the floor, covered by a white sheet. Only the soles of the man's shoes were visible.

The nursing supervisor with her ever-present clipboard was also in the room, along with one of the floor nurses. Neither spoke.

Deborah English, surrounded by support systems, lay on the bed.

"Well," Percy said, "I'd better take a look."

No one tried to talk him out of it. He gave them another minute, and still they said nothing; so he approached the body. He squatted—his bare ankles showing—and then waited a few seconds to make sure he wouldn't lose his balance and topple onto the body. He reached for a corner of the sheet.

Dead, definitely dead.

"What's his name?" he asked, his voice higher than normal.

"Gordon," the floor nurse said. "I don't know his last name."

"It'll say on his employee badge." The nursing supervisor poised her pencil as though to write down the information she expected *him* to get.

The smell was decidedly stronger, and not all that sweet in such close quarters. "The police will find that out," Smitson squeaked. He tossed the sheet back over the face and stood upright.

"The poor guy," Dr. Rojas said.

Percy hadn't actually touched him, but he wiped his hands, he hoped surreptitiously, on his slacks. "What killed him?"

Rojas pointed across the room, and Percy turned. A cardiac monitor sat several feet from the wall, its blue metal casing blistered and streaked with black. By the look of it, it was a relatively new piece of equipment. It was unplugged now, but it had to have been properly grounded and UL listed, he was sure.

"It caught on fire?" God, he hoped not, not with a file folder of reports regarding machine malfunctions sitting on his desk. There might be some liability here.

Rojas shrugged. "I don't know. Maybe the police or OSHA or our workman's comp carrier will figure it out. All I know is he got a jolt of current that would light a fair-sized city . . . and you saw what it did."

In spite of himself, Percy shuddered, remembering the man's eyes. The whites weren't white anymore, but rather a dark, turgid red.

He wanted to forget those eyes.

"This won't do," he said to himself.

Rojas gave him a questioning look. "Did you say something?"

"This won't do. This won't fucking do."

The nursing supervisor reacted to his obscenity as if she'd been slapped. The floor nurse covered her mouth with her hand, but her eyes showed amusement rather than shock. Rojas only shook his head.

"Well, I'd better get back to E.R." Rojas hitched up the pants of his greens.

The others filed out after the doctor. He thought he heard the floor nurse say something about lingerie, but figured he had to have misheard.

Percy stood with his hands on his hips and surveyed the room.

Was there a way to salvage this situation? Some way to lay the blame on that poor fool? After all, the guy was dead; what more could happen to him?

Maybe, he thought, I can tamper with the machine, shave some insulation off the power cord. Then sprinkle a little water on the floor. But no. Rojas had been in the room too long.

Rojas had probably been here since just after the

accident had occurred; not much got past him, Percy would wager.

Percy turned slowly in a full circle, his eyes searching the room, looking for anything that he could use. What else would account for an electrocution? Damn! He should have insisted the hospital's biomedical engineer check the equipment today—or rather yesterday—instead of waiting for next week.

And then he thought, What is to stop me from destroying the memo I sent agreeing to the delay? Then the engineer will take the fall.

"That's it," he said.

Belatedly he realized that he was alone with dead people. He glanced at Deborah English, a dead person who was breathing, and then scurried out of the room.

Twenty-One

After she woke up, it took Samantha a few minutes to get oriented to her surroundings.

Her room at the English house was bigger than the one at home, and the bed faced north rather than west, as she was used to. The light filtering through the shutters had a different quality to it, somehow paler.

She pushed the covers off her legs and sat up, running a hand through her short-cropped hair.

The clock on the bedside table showed it to be six A.M., early for her. She considered trying to get another thirty minutes of sleep, but doubted she'd be able to. It had taken forever to fall asleep last night.

It had always been that way with her; the lights went out and she replayed the day's events in her mind. On those occasions when something went bad, she tortured herself with doubts and recriminations. This time, why had she allowed Bronwyn to play on the slide in those slick-soled shoes?

She'd done a lot of tossing and turning before sleep claimed her.

At least, she thought, if I get up now, I'll be tired enough by bedtime to drop right off.

She got up and put on her robe, then went downstairs to put on the coffee so it would be ready when she got out of the shower.

Mrs. Henderson's kitchen was a model of efficiency, as expected. The coffee and filters were in a small cabinet directly above the automatic coffee maker, which was beside the sink. She wasted not a step or motion in setting it up.

Everything was like that: the plates and glasses were on the shelves above the dishwasher, with the silverware drawer to one side. Pots and pans hung on hooks, easily within reach of someone putting the clean dishes away.

Samantha remembered seeing a movie in which a character had the food in the cupboards arranged alphabetically. Mabel Henderson hadn't done that exactly, but never had Sam seen cans and boxes so neatly stored. All of the cans were lined up so that the pictures of the foods contained within faced forward.

The freezer, too, was organized, with carefully printed labels on each package. There were even "use by" dates on the meats.

Obviously, the housekeeper had stocked up before leaving on vacation. Sam smiled, wondering if the older woman really thought her so inept that she couldn't do something as simple as buying groceries.

If so, she could live with that; grocery shopping wasn't among her top ten favorite pastimes.

Sam had started out of the kitchen when she heard someone rapping at the back door. She turned, trying to remember whether Mrs. Henderson had mentioned anything about Saturday morning deliveries —she'd mentioned everything else—and then saw her own mother's face peering through the curtains.

"Mom?" She hurried to the door, unlocked it, and pulled it open. Her mother was wearing an old flannel robe and bedroom slippers, and her hair was still mussed from sleep. What could be urgent enough that she hadn't taken the time to dress before coming over? "What is it? Is something wrong?"

"Samantha, I just heard from Emily Whitaker that the little girl is in the hospital."

"Yes, but she's fine. They only kept her overnight for observation."

"Then it's true?"

Sam frowned; her mother's expression had grown more and not less concerned. "Yes, it's true."

"And you spent the night here?"

She looked down at her bare legs, and fingered the material of her robe. "No, Mom, I usually walk around in my nightclothes."

"Don't be fresh with me, young lady."

"I'm not trying to be fresh. Of course I spent the night here. I'm living here this summer, remember? You're the one who suggested I take the job."

"That was when I thought the little girl would be here with you."

"Her name is Bronwyn."

Mrs. Townsend waved an impatient hand. "I know her name—"

"Then use it, please. Anyway, she'll be home later today, and what difference does it make?"

"The difference is," her mother said, "that I don't want my daughter staying in a house alone—at night—with a man whose wife is . . . is . . ."

"Is what?"

A tinge of red appeared on her mother's cheeks and she lowered her voice. "Whose wife *isn't* able to take care of his . . . his . . ."

A light blinked on in Sam's mind. "Sexual needs?" she asked, as innocently as she could manage.

"Hush!" Her mother glanced over her shoulder, as though to make certain there was no one lurking in the nearby bushes who might overhear them. "But yes, if you want to put it that bluntly, his . . . yes."

It was difficult not to laugh at her mother's scandalized look or at the notion that Bronwyn's presence in the house would act as a talisman against sexual desire. "Well, Mom, nothing happened last night."

"You're sure?"

"Reasonably," Samantha said dryly.

"Thank heavens." Mrs. Townsend attempted a smile. "Now all we need to do is think of how to keep others from jumping to that conclusion."

The way my own mother did?

"Darn that Emily," Sam's mother said. "It would be so simple to say that I spent the night here, too; but she called on the stroke of six, and she knows good and well that she woke me up."

"Emily," Sam said, thoughtfully.

"Of course, it would be even better if we could say that Dr. English stayed at the hospital last night to be with the little . . . to be with Bronwyn. But the nurses would know better, and we all know how *they* like to talk."

"This whole town likes to talk."

Her mother either didn't hear or chose to ignore that. "Think, Samantha, think," she ordered. "What can we say happened?"

"How about the truth? That I spent the night in my room, and Wyatt spent the night in his."

"Wyatt?" The alarm returned to her mother's eyes in an instant. "It's Wyatt now?"

Sam sighed. "Mother."

"Listen, it's your reputation I'm concerned with. I'm only doing this for you."

"Well, don't."

"Samantha, you don't understand how people in this town are—"

"But I do. They're small-minded, parochial, mud-slinging fools. Wyatt is one of the finest men I know, and I don't mean in the Biblical sense, but even if I did, even if *we* did, I'm an adult now, and I'm responsible for my own behavior."

Her mother's eyes widened in shock. "What are you saying?"

"I'm not saying anything." Sam took her by the shoulders and turned her around, pointing her out the door. "Thank you for worrying about me, but I can take care of myself, and so can Wyatt."

"Wyatt," her mother murmured.

"And as for Emily, if I hear that she's said one word, *one word*, about either of us, there are a few things I can say about her."

"About Emily?"

"Definitely about Emily. Tell her that. Tell her that sometimes, say at a party, people think the kids are up in bed, but they've sneaked downstairs to see what's going on. And they do see what's going on, including things no one else sees."

"Oh my."

Seeing that she was in distress, Sam gave her mother a kiss. "Don't worry about it, Mom."

"I'll try not to," her mother said, looking doubtful.

"Good." She gave her a gentle push to start her on her way. "I love you, Mom."

The coffee had finished dripping by then, so Sam poured a cup and stood, leaning against the sink, sipping it slowly and wondering why people liked to talk trash. The nerve of Emily Whitaker, upsetting

169

her mother that way.

It wouldn't surprise Sam to learn that Emily had parked herself in the rose bushes, her binoculars trained at the windows all night long.

"Good morning."

Sam turned. Wyatt had come in without her hearing, and she felt a sense of relief that he hadn't come upon the scene with her mother. "Hi."

He was dressed casually in chinos and a short-sleeved blue shirt, but somehow on him the clothes looked rich. His dark hair was wet, not yet combed.

She was acutely aware of her own attire, or lack thereof.

"Coffee ready?"

"Sure." She got out of his way, sidestepping so closely that she could smell the scent of his aftershave. The effect was dizzying.

"Did you sleep well?" he asked, pouring coffee into a mug that bore the legend Daddy of the Year. Watching, she noticed that his wrists were slender for a man's, his hands strong but well shaped.

"Hmm? Oh, yes, fine," she lied. It was a good thing she hadn't known last night what the neighbors would be thinking this morning, or she'd never have gotten to sleep; she was perfectly capable of dreaming up her own fantasies about this man.

"I need to go to the office and catch up on some dictation. It shouldn't take more than a couple of hours. Then I'll stop by for you and we can go spring Bronwyn from the hospital."

"Sounds great."

He smiled at her, weakening her knees. "By the way, I never asked, but can you cook?"

"Cook? Ah . . . sure. I'm not a gourmet chef, but I get by. Do you want breakfast?"

"No, I was just wondering. Oh, and another thing.

170

we've all been invited to have dinner one night next week at Betty Cochran's."

"*We* have?" Betty Cochran was a viper in designer clothing. Sam found it hard to believe that woman would go to the trouble of asking Wyatt to dinner—she knew instinctively what was behind the invitation—and then include her.

"Yes. Is that all right with you, or would you rather have the night off?"

"No, I think I'd like to have dinner with you at Mrs. Cochran's."

That seemed to satisfy him, and he nodded. "Good. Well, I'd better be going."

Again he passed within inches of her, and she fought a civil war inside; her mother's daughter wanted her to take a step back, while *she* wanted to lean in toward him, perhaps brush against his arm. It ended in a standoff, and she remained where she was.

"I'll see you in a few hours," he said.

"I'll be ready."

Sam went upstairs and into the bathroom. She hung her robe on a hook on the door, pulled her thigh-length nightgown over her head, and turned on the shower.

It was the first time in her life she'd tried a cold shower, and it flat out didn't work.

Twenty-Two

Dr. Tony Armstrong felt a flash of irritation when he saw a patrol car parked in his assigned space. Then again, he had often harbored doubts as to whether the local boys in blue were able to read. For certain, they had a hard time writing; the last time he'd been caught speeding, it took the citing officer a solid ten minutes to laboriously write out the ticket.

Which had cost him eighty bucks.

He parked in Dr. Baylor's spot—Baylor never worked on Saturdays—and headed for the hospital's main entrance. A woman with two small children was in front of him, walking slowly so her toddlers could keep up, and he cut by them, glancing impatiently at his watch.

He had agreed to meet the EEG technician on West at eight A.M., and he knew better than to keep her waiting. Ever since he'd broken off their affair six months before, she had been acting as if she was doing him a favor by doing her job.

Normally he wouldn't take that attitude from anyone, and would put her in her place, but this little dolly was capable of calling his wife.

In retrospect, he should have known better than to

get involved with her; she wasn't his type at all. She was one of those big lusty blondes whose natural habitat was the beach, and who could drink him or any man under the table. The kind who, he thought unkindly, the years would turn frowzy.

She was destined to spend her forties and beyond perched on a bar stool, wearing a tube top and asking strange men to light her cigarettes.

She had a mouth on her, and said exactly what she thought, which initially he had found refreshing after twelve years of marriage to an ice princess who was genetically unable to express an opinion, if indeed she had one.

His life would be simpler if the woman were suddenly struck dumb.

Make that dumber.

Maybe today he would think of a way to convince her to let the past be past and to bury the hatchet, hopefully not in his back.

Armstrong had reached the corridor to West, and he quickened his pace.

"There you are," Jennifer said. "I thought you had stood me up."

"Am I late?" He wasn't, but didn't want to rile her. "I'm sorry."

"Really," she said, her tone flat. "Come on, then. Let's get this over with. I have other things to do today, you know."

"I appreciate your coming in." He noticed that the nurses were looking at him peculiarly, probably wondering why he was being so conciliatory, but he ignored them. "May I have Deborah English's chart?"

The secretary got it from the rack and handed it to

him without comment.

"Ladies first," he said, and smiled.

Jennifer quirked an eyebrow. "I don't see any 'ladies' around, Tony."

He hated it when she used his first name. "Shall we?"

"I think we already did," she said loud enough for everyone to hear, and then took off down the hall toward 6-West.

He followed after her, smoothing his razor-cut hair. He noticed two uniformed cops standing opposite Deborah's room. Both were watching Jennifer with obvious interest. From experience he knew she was putting on a show, with an extra wiggle in her walk.

Armstrong wanted to ask the cops if they were feeling suicidal, even thinking about bedding the bitch. But they'd taken his parking space; let them find out on their own, if they were so inclined.

Only when she'd disappeared into the room did their attention turn to him. He had a moment to wonder what they were doing here when a gurney bearing a black-bagged body was wheeled out of 6-West by two men whose IDs identified them as being from the coroner's office.

He looked at the body and frowned.

It was obviously too large to be Deborah English, so who was it?

"Who the hell is that?" he asked.

One of the coroner's men gave him a coolly measuring look. "Who are you?"

"I'm Dr. Armstrong. This"—he gestured—"is my patient's room."

"Well, Dr. Armstrong, there's been an accident." He nodded at the body. "The deceased appears to have been electrocuted."

"Electrocuted?" Armstrong could not keep from sounding incredulous.

"Yes, sir."

"In my patient's room?"

The man shrugged. "Anyway, we're through here, so we'll just get out of your way."

Armstrong watched them wheel the body down the hall, stopping briefly at the nurse's station before heading toward the front of the hospital. The morgue was located near pathology, and he supposed they were going there, since the coroner used the hospital's facilities to conduct autopsies.

Jennifer had come to stand beside him. "How much longer will you be?"

"They didn't tell me who that was," he said.

"Does it matter? You've seen one stiff, you've seen them all." She laughed her bawdy laugh. "And I should know, eh?"

That motivated him to go in the room.

One thing he'd have to give her; Jennifer was a skilled EEG tech. Not that it was that difficult a job, but she did it well. Within a few minutes, she had Deborah wired, and the electroencephalogram began.

Now that he had Wyatt English's permission to withdraw Deborah's support systems, he wanted to obtain verification that there had been no improvement in her brain-wave activity. It had been a number of months since he'd ordered an EEG on her, but that one had been essentially identical to those which had preceded it.

All displayed occasional flurries of electrical activity, but for the most part were nearly straight lines. None of the neurologists who had examined her EEGs over the years had been able to offer a cogent explanation for the peculiarly violent wave patterns, but the most frequently mentioned theory was that the waves represented interference from other sources.

It wasn't a theory he could agree with. The "other sources" referred to the machines and monitors which helped to sustain her, but all of the equipment was surge protected and filtered precisely to prevent such electrical interference.

There was also the fact that the wave patterns were markedly similar on all of the EEGs, from the first done eight years ago to the most recent and, no doubt, to the one Jennifer was obtaining now.

He hadn't a clue as to why it would be so, but he was comfortable with his assumption that her brain-wave patterns weren't medically significant. They were, he thought, a curiosity, and nothing more.

Regardless, he wanted documentation that nothing had changed.

"So," Jennifer said, disrupting his musings, "how's it hanging?"

Armstrong clenched his teeth to keep from telling her to shut her mouth. Remember the hatchet, he thought, and then said, "I've been fine. And you?"

"No one has ever complained," she smirked. "You didn't have any complaints, did you?"

"No." Not then.

"Good." She paused to write something on the graph paper. "And the lovely Mrs. Armstrong? How is she these days?"

"Fine, thank you." He opened the chart and began to page through it, hoping that Jennifer would respect his professional responsibilty to a patient and back off.

Apparently that was hoping too much. "Does she still have that little . . . problem?"

He pretended not to have heard, as though he was completely absorbed in reviewing the chart, but he knew what she was referring to. It had been a mistake to talk about his wife's sexual dysfunction with Jennifer, although they'd had a good laugh about it at the time.

Jennifer did not seem to be fooled. "You know, if you want, I could talk to her. Woman to woman. I mean, I do know something about it. I could give her a few tips, what do you say?"

Armstrong felt heat rise in his neck and knew that his ears must be fire-engine red. "I don't think that'll be necessary."

"Not necessary, maybe, but I do believe it would be enlightening for her."

"Don't threaten me," he said, his voice low. He went over and pushed the door closed. "I don't understand why you have to be so confrontational."

Jennifer laughed. "You mean bitchy."

"You knew when we started that nothing could come of it. I told you that."

"Yeah, well, that was then and this is now. Now I feel bitchy. I don't like being dumped."

You're going to make a career out of it, he thought. "I'm sorry if I hurt you—"

"Don't flatter yourself. I'm not hurt; I'm pissed off. And I'm tired of you doctors who think you can help yourself to the goodies without ever paying the price."

He regarded her for a moment. "What is the price?"

She made another notation on the graph paper. "I want a new car."

"A car."

"A Mercedes 450 SL. Convertible. Powder blue. White leather seats. Okay?"

It was blackmail, but what choice did he have? His wife would divorce him—and let the community property laws exact her revenge. Besides, he liked his life the way it was. And his wife, dysfunctional or not, was exquisite, which made him the envy of every man he knew.

So he said, "And you'll leave me alone after that."

"Oh, yes. I'll even call you *Dr*. Armstrong."

"All right. I'll see to it first thing on Monday."

She grinned. "See to it today," she said. "Remember, powder blue."

Armstrong stood at the bedside and contemplated his patient. The EEG had offered no surprises, but he hadn't expected it to.

This was the right decision, only it should have been made long ago. The woman was little more than a husk, empty and soulless. One had only to look in those clouded eyes to see the total nothingness she had become.

He'd never say so to Wyatt, but if it had been up to him, he would have done this years ago. His respect for his colleague had silenced him.

He wondered idly how long it would take her to finish dying, a process she'd started years ago.

The liquid feedings were to be stopped, and she would be taken off the ventilator. She breathed on her own, so the removal of the ventilator would have no immediate effect, but with the onset of pneumonia, its lack would speed the filling of her lungs.

She would either suffocate or starve.

Armstrong reached across and pinched the skin on her rib cage hard, twisting it almost viciously. Not even the tiniest reaction.

Satisfied, he turned and left the room.

179

Twenty-Three

Bronwyn made figure eights with her spoon through the oatmeal, stirring the raisins in.

She hadn't much appetite this morning. She'd woken feeling draggy, her muscles heavy and aching. The doctor in E.R. had told her that she'd be sore and stiff—"The second day is always worse," he'd said—but this was worse than worse.

The problem was, she was afraid that if she mentioned it to the nurse, the nurse would tell her doctor, and her doctor would make her stay in the hospital another day. She didn't want that.

She missed being home.

And after that dream last night, she was scared to be here.

Bronwyn lifted the spoon and guided it slowly to her mouth. The oatmeal was lukewarm. It hurt to swallow.

"How's your breakfast?"

A pink lady had appeared in the doorway, and was smiling at her with both upper and lower teeth.

"It's cold," she said, and pushed the bowl across the tray.

"Oh, dear, would you like me to warm it for you?

There's a microwave in the lounge."

Bronwyn shook her head as much as her neck would allow. "I'm not hungry."

"But you have to eat." The pink lady came to the bedside. "And breakfast is the most important meal of the day."

Mrs. Henderson had always said the same thing, but Bronwyn was unconvinced. Particularly since she'd never seen the housekeeper eat breakfast.

"Here, I'll warm this up. It'll only take a second."

She watched the pink lady hurry off with the oatmeal. It bothered her sometimes that adults didn't seem to listen to her. She knew that she didn't want the cereal, hot or cold. Why couldn't she decide for herself?

The best thing about growing up would be doing whatever she wanted.

Bronwyn folded her arms across her chest, feeling stubborn. She would *not* eat.

She glared in the direction of the doorway, waiting for the pink lady to return, but it was the nurse who came in, a small metal tray in her hand.

On the tray was a tiny white paper cup.

"Finished?" the nurse asked. Without waiting for an answer, she replaced the lid on the breakfast tray and pushed the table that held it off to one side. "I have your morning medication."

"I don't want it," Bronwyn said, transferring her anger from the pink lady to the nurse. "I hate taking pills."

"They're only aspirin, dear."

"That's worse." She'd stopped taking baby aspirin last year, which she'd been proud of at the time; but she couldn't swallow the bigger tablets easily, and more often than not they would start to dissolve while they were at the back of her throat. They tasted bitter and flaky, and they made her cough. "I don't want aspirin."

"Come on, Bronwyn. You said you had a headache this morning, and your doctor wants you to have the aspirin so it will go away."

"What *I* want is to go home," she said, and felt her lower lip begin to tremble.

The nurse's expression changed. "Poor baby. Of course you do. Your dad will be here soon—"

"When?"

"An hour or an hour and a half."

An hour was as long as forever, and a half an hour more would be more than she could bear. "I want to go home," she said. The edges of her vision blurred as tears gathered in her eyes.

The nurse put the paper cup containing the aspirin down and sat on the side of the bed. "Come on, honey, don't cry. Be a big girl."

She was so tired of being a big girl. She wanted to be a little girl, and have her daddy hold her in his lap and wipe away her tears. She wanted Homer to cuddle with, and her own pajamas, and especially not to be in this place anymore.

"Do you want me to call your father and ask if he can come and get you sooner?"

She nodded, too miserable to speak.

The nurse took a tissue from the small box on the bedside table and handed it to her. "Okay, honey, I'll go and call him right now."

After the nurse left, Bronwyn wanted to stop crying, but somehow she couldn't. She held the tissue over her mouth and sobbed into it.

Her head *was* throbbing, and crying made it hurt worse. Maybe she should have accepted the aspirin, but she wanted baby aspirin because right this minute she didn't care about being a big girl.

She hiccuped once and then again. The pain in her head was making her sick to her stomach, and now her nose was running.

Bronwyn curled up, lying on her side and hugging her knees to her, even though it stretched her tender muscles to do so. She closed her eyes and tried not to think about how bad she felt.

This must be what Mommy feels. Only she's never gonna get to go home.

The thought made her sad. It was something she'd known for a long time, but tried not to think about. Being in the hospital for one day was terrible; what must it be like to stay for years?

Her father had told her that her mother wasn't aware of anything, so her mother wasn't sad at what had happened to her, but Bronwyn didn't see how that could be. Even asleep last night, she'd known she wasn't in her own bed at home.

Wasn't a coma the same as being asleep?

Her tears had fallen onto the sheet, and her face was resting in the wet spot. She sniffled and tried again to stop, but her sobs seemed to start at a place deep within her and her whole body had begun to shake.

Now her ears began to ring, and she felt a kind of numbness spread over her scalp.

Where was the nurse?

Where was her father?

Where was her mother?

"Mommy," she cried, gasping. "Mommy, please come and take me home."

The numbness had reached her face, and she began to worry that she wouldn't be able to breathe. It felt as if her lungs wouldn't fill with air.

She was *so* sick, she couldn't even move, and then through the roaring in her ears, she heard someone come into her room.

Twenty-Four

"She's fine," the nurse on the medical floor said in answer to his question.

"What happened?"

"The poor little darling was homesick, and she started to cry—"

"That isn't like Bronwyn," Wyatt interrupted. She hadn't even cried yesterday after having fallen from the slide.

"Well, apparently she had a nightmare last night, and this morning she woke up with a headache. I offered her an aspirin, but she wouldn't take it. She started crying, as I said, and when I left to call you, I imagine she started to hyperventilate."

"I see."

"It scared her even more, of course, and she got a little panicky, and . . ." She gestured as if to say, what could I do?

Wyatt knew hyperventilating was an experience that even frightened adults. There was a sensation of not being able to breathe, which caused the sufferer to take more frequent breaths. The reduction of carbon dioxide in the blood produced a lowering of blood pressure, dizziness, and vasoconstriction.

It also induced anxiety, and frequently resulted from it as well.

"I had her breathe into a brown paper bag and held her hand until she calmed down," the nurse added, "and she finally fell asleep."

Sam, who'd been standing by quietly, asked, "She's all right, then?"

"Oh yes, she's fine."

Wyatt detected something in the nurse's eyes that made him uneasy. "Is that all?"

The nurse hesitated. "There was . . . I don't know how to explain this."

"Go on," he prompted.

"It was the strangest thing. I had just come back to the room after speaking to you and saw at once that she was in some distress, when they called a 'Doctor Stat' over the intercom."

Doctor Stat was an urgent call for any available doctor in the hospital to assist in a code situation. It was the rough equivalent of a Code Blue, the most serious of the assistance-required codes.

"And?"

"And she was convinced, the poor child, that the call was for her, and that she was dying."

It made a kind of perverse sense. Bronwyn knew very well what a Doctor Stat was for, and in her panicked state of feeling herself unable to breathe, it might very well have occurred to her that the call *was* for her.

"The poor kid," Sam said.

"She kept saying, 'Help me' and crying, and calling for you and . . . and her mother."

Wyatt frowned. "She called for her mother?"

The nurse knew, as everyone in the hospital did, about Deborah. "Yes. She was frightened, I suppose."

186

"I don't blame her." He hesitated. "About the nightmare she had . . . what do you know?"

"Only what the night nurse told me. She said she heard Bronwyn whimpering and went into the room to check on her. Apparently, she had kicked off the covers, and she was lying there shivering."

That concerned him almost as much as this morning's episode.

"I gather that Bronwyn wasn't fully awake, but she complained of being cold and of someone being in her room." The nurse smiled faintly. "Which of course is the most common nightmare we hear of in the hospital. The patients aren't used to people moving about at night while they're sleeping, and they incorporate their uneasiness at the loss of privacy into the dream. And it's possible that someone *may* have gone into her room, although none of the nurses could recall doing so."

All of it was plausible, Wyatt knew, but for some reason he felt apprehensive.

"As for being cold, well, she'd kicked the covers all the way off the bed."

He thought of what Eva had said about Bronwyn having nothing to fear at being in the hospital, and realized how little adults remembered about a child's mind. Obviously, this hadn't been a pleasant experience.

"Has her doctor been in to see her this morning?"

The nurse nodded. "As it happens, he got here a few minutes later, but he went off to the Doctor Stat. When he came back he checked her over, and he's signed her discharge papers."

"So she can go home?" Sam asked.

"Yes."

Sam looked at Wyatt. "Do you think we should

187

wake her up?"

"It might be a good idea." He touched her hand. "Sam, you go in and I'll be there in a minute."

"Sure." She smiled jauntily and went off down the hall.

He waited until she'd disappeared into the room, then turned again to the nurse. "Is that everything?" he asked, unable to shake the feeling that there was something he wasn't being told.

"It's everything that concerns your daughter."

Her tone was guarded, careful, and it told him there was more. "What is it?"

"Last night, Dr. English, one of the hospital employees, a janitor, was killed in your wife's room."

"What?" The sharpness of the word cut through the murmur of other conversations, and all of the nurses at the station focused their attention on him.

"I really don't know much more than that. I heard that he was electrocuted."

Wyatt shook his head.

"I think they suspect that one of the machines in the room shorted out when he went to move it so that he could wax the floor."

One of the other nurses spoke up: "The supervisor said it was the cardiac monitor. It blew him right out of his shoes."

"Jesus," Wyatt said. In all of his years in medicine, he'd never heard of anything like that happening. He would have thought it an impossibility.

"It's very sad," another nurse said.

"Was that the stat call?"

Bronwyn's nurse's face clouded. "No, that was something even worse."

He waited for her to continue.

"It was for one of the doctors."

Last year an anesthesiologist had suffered a massive cardiac infarction, and had keeled over in the operating room. In an incident which had become near legend, the radiologist had run out into the hall, yelling, "Get a doctor, somebody call a doctor."

The anesthesiologist had recovered, but the incident had become the source of a lot of sick jokes around the hospital, which already abounded with the black humor common to those who worked in high-stress, life-or-death situations. There was no shortage of skilled mimics who had come to rely on a reenactment of the radiologist's actions for a guaranteed laugh.

Whatever had happened this morning, it was too fresh to be subject to that process of letting off tension; the nurses' faces were grim.

"It was Dr. Armstrong," someone said.

Wyatt felt as though he'd been struck; he'd talked to Tony only yesterday. "It can't be. What . . . do you know what happened?"

"No one is saying."

"But—"

He was interrupted by the call over the intercom: "Doctor Stat to the Emergency Room, please," the voice said, "Doctor Stat to the Emergency Room."

Without another word Wyatt took off running down the hall toward the front of the hospital.

The place was a madhouse. The ambulance bay doors were open and at least two ambulances were backed up to it. The EMTs were carting stretcher after stretcher of injured into the department.

The E.R. doctor and a nurse were conducting triage, routing the patients to treatment areas according to severity of injury.

"What've you got?" he asked a passing EMT.

"Eight victims from a head-on collision out on Coast Road."

"Wyatt," the E.R. doctor said, "take this one in the code room, will you?"

He didn't even answer, but grabbed hold of a stretcher handle and began to pull it along into the assigned room. A nurse who usually worked ICU tagged behind.

The patient was a young female, perhaps sixteen or seventeen, and she was covered in blood. She was dressed in a T-shirt and shorts, and one foot had a sandal on it. Her shoulder-length hair was wet with blood, plastered to her head.

Road burns covered her right side from shoulder to knee, and bits of gravel were embedded in her flesh which was seeping blood and serum.

Her face, pale beneath the spatters of blood, was scored with dozens of tiny cuts and one large V-shaped laceration on her right cheekbone. The skin flapped open as her head moved in the throes of her distress. She was not conscious, but she was making a low, moaning sound in her throat.

Her respiration was labored and shallow.

The EMTs had established an IV line which was running wide open with a thousand cc's of Ringer's solution. They had placed a splint on her right leg to immobilize it; he could see white splinters of bone protruding through the abraded skin.

The nurse was already cutting the girl's clothes off her.

Wyatt took a penlight to check her pupillary responses, flashing it and noting the sluggishness of the left eye. The right was dilated and nonresponsive, indicative of brain damage. The first indications of decerebrate rigidity was evidenced by the clenching of her jaw and retraction of the neck muscles.

All of which were ominous signs; the girl's prognosis wasn't good.

"She'll need a neurosurgeon," he said. "But for now, let's get her stabilized."

This was the so-called "Golden Hour" in medicine, the first sixty minutes after a severe injury when doctors had the best chance to save a life.

Wyatt had a strong suspicion that in this case, he would fail.

He lost track of time.

The girl had been taken to Intensive Care, and would be placed on a respirator. He had moved on to the next patient, a fourteen-year-old boy whose outcome looked decidedly better.

They'd had to tie the boy's arms and legs to the rails of the gurney, because he was somewhat combative. He smelled of beer and urine—he'd become incontinent after the accident—and he kept trying to sit up.

"Take it easy," Wyatt said, pressing his shoulders down on the bed.

"Shit, what happened," the boy said, slurring his speech. One of his teeth had been knocked loose and his mouth had dried blood in the corners. His forehead was skinned up a bit, and two of the fingers on his left hand were broken and displaced.

But that was the worst of it; he'd been incredibly lucky.

"Where's my friends? What happened to my friends?"

The nurse was cutting through the thick denim of his jeans and having a difficult time with the wet material. She made a face. "Be still now, will you?"

With all the bluster he could manage, he swore. "Damn it, I want to know what happened to my friends."

"There's been an accident," Wyatt said.

"I know that, I was there, man." He tried to free his arms of the restraints. "What *is* this? Why can't I get up? Where's Todd?"

Wyatt and the nurse exchanged a look. Todd had been the driver of the four-wheel-drive vehicle with five kids as passengers. None were wearing seat belts. Todd had died at the scene.

Of the family of three in the other car, only the child, a three-year-old, had been seriously injured. The parents were buckled in, but the child had been standing on the back seat. The force of the collision had catapulted him through the windshield.

Wyatt was thankful that he hadn't been asked to work on the three-year-old. It was bad enough having to see that small battered body.

"Todd's dad is gonna kill him," the boy said from out of nowhere, "for wrecking the Jeep."

The radiology technician had arrived with the lumbering portable X-ray machine. Wyatt left the treatment room, since the patient was stable and there was hardly space for the machine and the gurney.

The E.R. doctor looked up wearily as he approached the department office.

"Thanks," he said.

Wyatt dropped into the chair beside him. "What's the final toll?"

He sighed. "The little boy isn't going to make it, but I don't think anyone expected him to. The parents have agreed to donate his organs; there's a transplant team from Loma Linda on the way."

192

"Ah . . . damn."

"The girl you worked on, well, you know. We haven't been able to notify her family yet." He scratched his nose. "And I had a nineteen-year-old male, so far a John Doe, who is in surgery with a ruptured aortic aneurysm. If he pulls through, I'll be very, very surprised."

"The others?"

"Two have been admitted, a third is going into O.R.—when it's free—for a closed reduction of a tibia-fibula fracture, and the other two are still here."

"Well, the boy I've got can probably be discharged after the orthopedic surgeon reduces his fractures and puts a cast on his hand." Wyatt smiled grimly. "And after he sobers up."

"God, what a day."

"Excuse me, Dr. English?" The department secretary had come up beside them. "I have a message for you from the medical floor. They said to tell you that a Miss Townsend has taken your daughter home."

Wyatt glanced at the wall clock and was startled to see that more than three hours had gone by. He reached for the phone, intending to call home.

"You know, Wyatt," the E.R. doctor said, "I'm worried what all of this is going to do to our plans for a trauma unit."

"It should make a strong case," he said as he dialed. "We were seriously underequipped and understaffed."

"Yeah, but you know Smitson. He'll say that we got by with the facilities we have, and argue that the lives we lost would have been lost anyway."

The phone was ringing. "He can say that, but no one can know for sure." The line had rung six times. He counted four more and then returned the receiver to the cradle. He would finish up here and go straight home.

"The little bastard ought to be the one who gets to tell those kids' parents that they died. That might jar loose a bit of human compassion."

"I wouldn't bet on it," Wyatt said. "But he'd best stop putting roadblocks in our way, or there'll be another head-on collision."

Twenty-Five

Cassie Owens listened, fascinated, as the day supervisor described the two deaths that had occurred on their shift, the second of which—Dr. Armstrong's —the supervisor had witnessed.

"I saw him in the hall and asked him if he would mind taking a look at Mr. Viola in 3-West."

Viola, Cassie knew, was the gentleman who'd been diagnosed as a catatonic following a schizophrenic episode eighteen months ago, during which he'd attacked his wife with a ball-peen hammer.

She'd never been assigned as his nurse, which was fine with her, because he gave her the creeps. The few times she'd seen him, she was certain that his eyes were following her.

"Mr. Viola's rash has gotten worse, despite the hydrocortisone cream his own doctor prescribed, and I wanted someone to check him, because the pustules had begun to suppurate."

Cassie rolled her eyes heavenward. Why, she wondered, couldn't anyone use simple words? Why not come right out and say his rash was oozing pus?

"Dr. Armstrong suggested that we try a different medication, perhaps triamcinolone ointment or

Fluocinonide, and I went to the drug cabinet to see what we had on hand."

"Which was nothing," someone behind Cassie said.

"When I came back, not more than two or three minutes later, I found Mr. Viola standing—yes, *standing* over Dr. Armstrong."

"I knew it," one of the nurses said. "Here I've been lifting that boneless wonder in and out of bed for all this time, busting my buns, and he can stand."

The supervisor held her hand up for quiet, her expression reproving. "He was standing over Dr. Armstrong, who was on the floor, and he had the paddles of the portable defibrillator poised on either side of the doctor's head. I said, 'Mr. Viola, what are you doing?'"

Someone snickered.

"Dr. Armstrong said, 'Stay calm and get Security.'"

"Oh, *that* would help."

Cassie turned to see who'd spoken and wasn't surprised at all to see it was an ICU nurse who floated to West once or twice a month. The Intensive Care nurses tended to consider themselves the *crème de la crème* of the staff, which perhaps explained their big mouths.

"If the security guards actually had to do something like restrain a patient," the ICU nurse continued, "they'd probably drop dead in their tracks."

Cassie hated, on principle, to agree with her, but she'd often thought the same thing; to a man the guards were overweight, slow, and timid. Some of the nurses asked the guards to walk them to their cars at night, but unless the idea was for the guard to faint and create a diversion so the nurse might escape an attacker, she didn't know what use they'd be.

"If you don't mind," the supervisor said coldly,

losing patience at last, "I'd like to go on with what I was saying."

No one spoke.

"All right, then. As I said, Dr. Armstrong asked me to call for help, and I started to back out of the room. Then Mr. Viola hit the discharge button and . . . and . . ."

"Fried his brains." Another whisper from the back of the room.

"He just kept doing it, again and again, until the defibrillator hadn't any wattage left." The nursing supervisor closed her eyes and placed her hand over her mouth.

Cassie could see that the woman was swallowing repeatedly, obviously in an attempt to keep from being sick. She felt slightly nauseated herself.

"It was terrible," the supervisor said when she regained control. "Dr. Armstrong must have been dead by the second or third shock, don't you think?"

A few of the nurses nodded, but Cassie wasn't sure. When she was in nursing school, an intern, fooling around one night, had done much the same thing to himself, and it had only knocked him out—and melted the metal frames of his glasses.

Of course, he'd never been the same afterward.

The first shock had probably either stunned Dr. Armstrong or knocked him out. She hoped it had knocked him out; the thought of anyone being conscious and waiting for a second jolt was truly terrifying.

"I have to admit," the supervisor said, "I couldn't move. I couldn't do a thing to stop Mr. Viola. I couldn't help Dr. Armstrong."

"What happened then?" the ICU nurse asked.

"Mr. Viola dropped the paddles, went back to his chair by the window, sat down, and hasn't moved since. He never said a word, never even blinked."

A murmur passed among them.

"My first reaction was that it wasn't real, that I'd imagined it, but there was the doctor, lying dead on the floor."

"How horrible," someone said.

"I'm not even sure who it was that called in the Doctor Stat."

The day-shift unit secretary, who never before had been present at Report, said, "It was the EEG technician; I think her name is Jennifer."

"Was it?"

"She came running up to the desk, grabbed the phone and said, 'My car, there goes my car.'"

"What did she mean by that?"

The secretary shrugged. "Who knows? I heard her ask the operator to page a Doctor Stat to West, and I went looking for the crash cart." She paused. "What was it doing by Viola's room anyway? That's not where it's kept."

"They were going to move the equipment Dr. Armstrong had ordered discontinued from Mrs. English's room," the supervisor said, "and so they pushed the crash cart down to three to get it out of their way."

"And into Mr. Viola's way," Cassie said thoughtfully.

"Exactly," the secretary said.

After finishing Report, Cassie went to check Deborah English's chart. There, in his neat hand—uncharacteristic for a doctor—were the last orders Dr. Armstrong ever wrote.

It gave her an odd feeling to read them, knowing that within minutes of finishing them, he was dead. Dead, as the saying went, before the ink was dry.

The orders, however, had been carried out. The day nurse's initials appeared beside each one.

The nasogastric feeding tube had been removed. The last feeding had been the one Cassie had given yesterday.

The ventilator had been disconnected, and the patient was now on room air, breathing unassisted.

With the exception of the cardiac monitor, all other telemetry equipment had been discontinued. The alarm on the cardiac monitor had been disabled; nurses tended to respond to alarms almost on a knee-jerk level, as in resuscitate now, regret it later.

All medications had been stopped.

The arms boards and other restraining devices, including her jaw brace, had been removed.

Only the catheter remained in place.

Vital signs were to be taken q four hours. The one P.M. vitals showed that her temperature was hovering still in the vicinity of a hundred and three degrees. Blood pressure was low at ninety over sixty. Respirations were rapid at thirty breaths per minute, and labored, which they should be if she was developing a full-blown pneumonia.

What it came down to was that Deborah English was to receive only compassionate care. If she showed any signs of distress—which was unlikely—there was an order for morphine sulfate.

This, Cassie knew, was one way to hurry the end along. It would depress her respirations, and quite possibly kill her outright in her weakened state.

Dr. Armstrong had thought of everything.

She was glad the nursing supervisor hadn't run into him until after he'd written the orders.

Cassie closed the chart, and got up to start her evening's work.

Twenty-Six

Sam sat on the couch with Bronwyn stretched out beside her and watched the sleeping child's face. The poor kid had barely lasted through dinner, her eyelids at half-mast and her responses just a little slow, as though she were moving through molasses.

Even so, she'd insisted on staying up to watch a Charlie Brown special on TV. She had turned off the lamps so the room was lit only by the flickering of the set, and had made herself comfortable, but within moments of resting her head in Sam's lap, she'd drifted off to sleep.

Sam brushed the soft hair back from the small, pale face, and thought she understood for the first time how a mother must feel.

Wyatt returned from making a call to the hospital, and he smiled when he saw them, the tension vanishing from his face. "It's true what they say about how children look like angels when they sleep, isn't it?"

"It's true about this child, anyway."

He sat at the end of the couch, resting his hand on Bronwyn's stockinged foot. "She's so much like her mother," he said.

Sam heard the sadness in his voice, and wished she knew what to say to comfort him. Maybe the thing to do was say nothing, but almost without thinking, she heard herself ask, "Is it difficult for you? That Bronwyn resembles your wife?"

He didn't answer immediately, and she thought that he might not. Had she offended him, asking such a personal question?

"It was at first," he said then. He was looking in her direction, but not at her, as if he were seeing into the past. "There were times, in the months after she was born, when I couldn't bear to go into the nursery, couldn't bear to pick her up and hold her, because she reminded me of how much I had lost. I busied myself in work, and sometimes wouldn't come home for days."

"That must have been terrible for you."

"Not terrible as much as frightening. I was scared half out of my mind that I wouldn't be able to be a good father to her."

"You're a great father," Sam said, remembering the sprinklers.

He seemed not to have heard. "Deborah wanted to have a child so badly. The day she found out she was pregnant she was as beautiful as I'd ever seen her. She had this . . . this look about her. More than a glow. A glow doesn't even begin to describe it." A smile played at the corners of his mouth. "I teased her, saying the way she was acting you would think no woman had ever been pregnant before."

Sam felt her breath catch in her throat, putting herself in Deborah's place.

"She hadn't had a family of her own. No one knew who her father was, and her mother disappeared shortly after she was born, never to be heard from again."

"There weren't any relatives, or anyone to take her in?"

"Just an aunt, I think, but she was elderly and unwilling to take on the expense and trouble of raising a child."

"How sad."

"The county, of course, assumed custody."

"She wasn't adopted?"

He shook his head. "It was strange, the way it happened. Deborah was born in a small town, smaller than Hansen's Point, amazing as that may seem, up near the Oregon border. The woman the county appointed as guardian was, from what Deborah told me, a rather eccentric lady who ran a church-sponsored home for wayward girls."

"That's odd," Samantha said. "Why would they put a baby in a place like that?"

"There wasn't much choice. It was either that or ship her off to the big city—San Francisco, I assume—and they were loath to do that."

Sam glanced down at Bronwyn, who had shifted position in her sleep. She continued stroking her hair.

"Anyway, there weren't many parental prospects in a town that size, and the few who inquired about Deborah, the guardian turned down. She would say they weren't responsible enough or they weren't financially stable. Sometimes, from what Deborah told me, she simply said no without offering a reason at all."

"She had that much authority?"

"She must have. Apparently her brother was a circuit judge, and he was there to back her up. Whatever the cause, Deborah grew up in a home for wayward girls. The girls came and went, but Deborah stayed on. She left when she was eighteen."

"No one knew why," Sam asked, "this woman, her guardian, wanted to keep her?"

"Deborah said that the woman used her as a warning to the girls."

"What?"

"She made the girls take turns caring for Deborah, so that they would see what it would be like having babies of their own. She was kind of a deterrent, I suppose. Have sex and this will be your life, changing diapers, washing bottles, and waking up in the middle of the night to care for a crying baby."

"She wasn't a baby for eighteen years," Sam pointed out reasonably.

"No, but for long enough to make her less attractive as an adoption prospect. How many parents would want to adopt a three- or four-year-old who'd been raised, essentially, by the 'bad girls' in town?"

"I can't believe someone could get away with that, depriving a child of the right to have a good home. It's immoral."

"Or amoral. I felt the same way when Deborah told me. I wanted to go find the woman and read her the riot act, but I never did."

Sam was silent for a moment, thinking what it might have been like to grow up that way. "Was she . . . bitter about her childhood?"

"I honestly don't know. When she told me, she was very matter-of-fact about it. She didn't want sympathy, that was clear. I had a friend at the time who went on to become a psychiatrist, and he suggested to her that she had buried her rage, and that one day, if she didn't deal with it, it might blow up in her face."

"How did you meet?"

He laughed, and the memory transformed him; he looked younger, and carefree. "I was doing the first

204

year of my residency, working thirty-six-hour shifts, and little else. One day I had gotten off work and was walking to my apartment, which was about two blocks from the hospital. There was a small park in the neighborhood, and I would take a shortcut through it to save a few minutes of time—every minute saved was a minute I could sleep—and in the middle of the park was an old oak. And this day I saw there was a small crowd of people around the tree, along with guys wearing hard hats."

"Oh no. They were going to cut it down?"

Wyatt nodded. "That was the plan, but they hadn't reckoned on Deborah."

Samantha smiled in anticipation.

"There she was, sitting up in the tree." He laughed again. "She'd kicked off her shoes and climbed up in the branches, and she wasn't going to come down, she said, until they promised to leave the tree standing."

"Did they?"

"If they hadn't"—his voice lowered and she heard it catch—"she'd still be there."

"Oh . . ."

He looked at Bronwyn, his hand closing gently around her foot, and it was a moment before he looked up again. "So . . . when it came time to get down, she wasn't as sure how to go about it—she was wearing a dress—and so I did the gallant thing and went up after her."

"That is so romantic," Sam whispered.

"I'd never seen anyone so beautiful. I thought I'd found a wood nymph, a mythical creature who might not be real. Her hair was tousled, kind of wild, and she was flushed with excitement. I think I fell in love with her before we'd even spoken a word."

"And?"

205

"And I nearly got us both killed coming down out of that tree. All I could think about was how it felt to touch her, and that I never wanted to stop. . . ."

"But you got down."

"Eventually." He grinned ruefully. "A policeman had arrived, and there was no way I was going to let him rescue the both of us."

"Then what happened?"

"I took her out to lunch, and that was that. I never got to sleep that day."

"And you . . . were married." She'd started to say lived happily ever after but that wasn't how the story ended. Her throat ached at how he must be feeling right now.

"Three years later, when I finished my residency. And two years after that, Bronwyn was born."

Five years, she thought, they only had five years.

Neither of them spoke for several minutes. On the television, the credits for Charlie Brown were rolling. She saw them through a blur.

"Well," he said finally, "I'd better carry her upstairs and put her to bed."

"I'll help," Sam said.

She found a clean pair of pajamas in the top drawer of Bronwyn's dresser and brought them to the bed.

Wyatt had taken off his daughter's socks but was having a difficult time with her new jeans.

"Let me," Sam said. In a few seconds she had them off, and was working on the T-shirt. Bronwyn stirred but didn't waken.

"She must be tired," Wyatt said. "She's not usually this sound a sleeper. When I come home after having been called to the hospital, she hears me

206

and gets up."

"Nightmares have a way of ruining your sleep." Sam slipped the pajama top over the child's head, then guided her arms through the sleeves. "I asked her about that this afternoon."

"Her nightmare?"

"Yes. I thought she might want to talk about it."

"Did she?"

Sam frowned. "Yes and no. She said that someone was in her room, talking to her, but she wouldn't tell me what was said."

"Maybe she doesn't know. I can't remember most of my dreams."

"Maybe." Sam finished dressing Bronwyn, and pulled the covers over her. "I think she remembers and doesn't want to tell anyone."

"Why do you say that?"

"It's hard to explain. But I had the impression that she was protecting someone."

Wyatt shook his head. "I don't understand. Who would she be protecting?" He snapped off the light at the bedside and leaned down to kiss his daughter good night.

Sam didn't answer, the question driven from her mind as she watched father and child in the dim light, and felt an ache inside that was quickly becoming familiar.

I'm not going to want to leave when the summer's over.

She followed him from the room, but as he stopped and reached behind her to close the door, she put her hand on his arm.

"Leave it open," she said. "I want to be able to hear her if she cries out."

*   *   *

207

At nine o'clock, Wyatt took another call from the hospital and left.

Samantha wandered through the silent house, stopping at each of the windows and gazing out, studying the shadows, although she couldn't have said why.

Twenty-Seven

Lucille Morris put the lab tray on the counter of the nursing station on West and began thumbing through her stack of requisitions.

"Who are you here for?" the unit secretary asked.

"Hold on and I'll tell you." She picked two out of the pile. "English and Randall."

"English?" One of the nurses swiveled in her chair. "What are you drawing English for?"

"The third of three blood cultures."

The nurse—Lucille now recognized her as Owens —started shaking her head. "There must be some mistake. Dr. Armstrong canceled all of that, I'm sure."

"If he did, the lab didn't get wind of it." Lucille paused. "Wasn't that something, the way he died?"

Owens ignored that, and got up to take a look at the lab slip. "You don't have to do this one," she said, and made as though to tear it in half.

"Wait a minute." Lucille plucked it out of Owens's hands. "I do have to do it, unless you've got a written order not to."

The nurse looked exasperated, but went over and grabbed the chart.

"Have you heard anything more about Armstrong?" Lucille asked the secretary.

"Nope. They're going to do an autopsy tomorrow—"

"On a Sunday?"

"That's what I hear." The secretary leaned forward, shielding her mouth with her hand. "They're running out of space to put the bodies."

"I hadn't thought about that," Lucille said, "but you must be right. There are, what? Four drawers?"

"Right. And they're full. There's that janitor who was killed on the graveyard shift, Dr. Armstrong, and those two from the auto accident this afternoon."

"Oh, the girl died then? I knew the driver bought it—and it serves him right, doing eighty on a windy road, the stupid little jerk—but the last I heard the girl was in ICU. I've got an order to draw a CBC on her."

"She died a few minutes ago."

"Huh. How about that."

Neither of them mentioned the three-year-old who this very minute was probably being wheeled into O.R. where a transplant team would take his heart, lungs, liver, kidneys, and corneas.

A three-year-old body wouldn't take up much space in the morgue, anyway.

Owens came back, and she didn't appear to be pleased. I can't find an order canceling the blood cultures, so you might as well go ahead and do it, even if it is a waste of time," she said, and walked away.

Lucille shrugged. "Listen, it's not my idea," she called after her, "but if I'm not here drawing blood, I've got to be back in the lab taking blood donations." The nurse had disappeared from sight, so she addressed the secretary, "And I'd rather do this."

"You're *still* taking donations, at this hour? It's ten o'clock."

"Well, I'm not, but the lab is. We had no choice; the guy with the aneurysm nearly wiped us out single-handed. We called around to other hospitals to get more, but no one has blood to spare. It's summertime. The supply is always down, and the need is always up."

"Heavens, where do you find people willing to give a pint of blood on a Saturday night?"

"It's not that hard. The high-school football team is always good for it—the boys like to think they're so macho that their blood is better than anyone else's—and the rest are either hospital employees or regular donors we called in."

The secretary rubbed at the crook of her elbow. "I may be a rotten person, but I don't think I could donate blood to save my own mother's life."

"It's not so bad. As a matter of fact, I'm going to let them bleed me for a pint after I finish my rounds."

"Ugh." She shuddered. "It gives me the willies even hearing it. Blood, ugh."

"You sure picked a great place to work if blood makes you sick."

"It's only *my* blood that makes me sick. Anyone else's I can take, but watching my own blood being drawn out of my veins . . . ugh."

Lucille laughed. "Hey, if I give blood, they'll let me lie there for twenty minutes or so, and then I get to go home early. It's worth it," she said, and grabbed her tray. "See you."

She drew Randall first because he had those bulging veins that a blind man could stick on the first try. She collected four vials of blood within a minute, and then had a heck of a time trying to stop the bleeding. Randall had been getting blood thinners—anticoagulants—for his phlebitis, but this was the first time she'd had trouble with excessive bleeding.

It took five minutes of standing with her thumb over the puncture wound before it stopped spurting. Rather than use a Band-Aid, Lucille wadded up a gauze pad and taped it to his arm securely.

"That ought to hold you," she said.

She went into 6-West next, and was mildly surprised to see that most of the support equipment had been removed. Only one of the smaller cardiac monitors was in use. The blue line on the screen seemed irregular and a little fast, but what did she know? She wasn't a nurse.

Everyone in lab hated to draw English, whose veins were constricted and had been known to roll out of the needle's path.

Her own method was to use the blood-pressure cuff as the tourniquet, since she could pump it up much tighter than she could pull the rubber tie. It wasn't quite kosher as far as technique went, and she supposed if the woman had any feeling left it would be very uncomfortable, but she figured, what the hell. Who was going to complain?

No one.

Lucille got the cuff from its little basket on the wall and wrapped it snugly around the patient's upper arm. As thin as Deborah English was, she would have used a child-sized cuff if she'd had one.

She pumped the cuff up to over two hundred and tightened the small wheel to keep it inflated. Then she used her index and middle fingers to palpate a vein.

When she had located a likely spot, she turned and

grabbed a sealed sterile venipuncture needle. After tearing off the wrapping, she removed the sheath and positioned the needle above the vein.

"Here we go, let's get it on the first stick, shall we?" she asked the motionless patient.

But she didn't. The vein rolled and she merely nicked it. "Damn it." Rather than withdraw the needle, she moved it around, prodding and pushing until she felt it was on target.

This time she hit it, and a dark droplet of blood appeared on the stylet.

She inserted a vial with a black rubber stopper and watched it fill with blood. With the added pressure from the blood-pressure cuff, it went almost as quickly as Randall's draw.

She noticed, however, that the first stick was going to leave a bruise. Unfortunately, the same pressure that worked for her in getting a fast draw was also responsible for leaking quantities of blood into the soft tissue of the patient's arm.

Down in the lab they called her "Bruising Lucy" because of this exact thing. She took their ribbing good-naturedly, but one of these days, she'd like to get it right.

"Are they gone?" she asked Marcia when she returned to the lab.

"They?"

"The blood donors."

"Oh, yeah." Marcia grinned. "Timed it just right, didn't you?"

"Absolutely." Lucille put her tray on the desk and gathered up all of the vials and the accompanying paperwork. She carried them to the metal "in" rack and lined them up. The glass slides that she'd prepared, she put in a second cardboard tray.

"So, do you still want to donate a pint of O?"

"But of course. That is, if you still have any orange juice left." It was policy to give blood donors a small cup of OJ after they'd been bled. "And especially if you'll put a jigger of vodka in it."

"Sorry, all out of vodka."

It was the departmental joke, worn a bit thin from overuse, but who was she to flaunt tradition?

Lucille hopped up on one of the padded tables, and rolled up the sleeve of her uniform. Marcia brought over the blood-collection kit and began to set up.

"They told me over on West that the girl from the accident died," she said, "so I didn't get over to ICU. Have you heard anything new about the boy with the aneurysm?"

Marcia wiped her arm with alcohol and then Betadine. "He's hanging in."

"I wonder if they're going to transfer him."

"I doubt that, at least for the time being. I think they're afraid to move him. If the resection of that aneurysm blows, he could be dead in ten minutes flat." Marcia secured the tourniquet and then gently slapped her arm to bring the vein up.

"Have they identified him yet?" Lucille was talking to keep from feeling the sting of the needle, but when it pierced her skin she winced. "Ouch."

"Sorry. No, he's a John Doe for now. None of the other kids in the Jeep know who he is; he was hitchhiking and they'd picked him up."

"And gave him a ride to the end of the line." Lucille sighed. "Oh well, we all gotta go sometime."

"Okay, you're off and running. I'll be back to check on you in a while."

"Take your time; I'm a slow bleeder." She closed

214

her eyes. "And I think I'll take a little nap."

Lucille was drifting in and out of sleep, feeling as though she were floating. The sounds of the hospital—the intercom, voices, the hum of the air conditioner—faded away.

She had a tingling feeling in her hands, and it almost brought her awake. But somehow the effort was too much. All she wanted to do was sleep.

Her ears began to ring, which annoyed her, and then she became aware of a dripping sound. Had someone left a faucet running?

Slowly, Lucille opened her eyes and turned her head to the side. The movement made the room spin, and she found that it was difficult to focus.

What was that dripping?

The lab seemed to be awfully dark, and she wondered if . . . if . . . what was her name? Marcia. She wondered if Marcia had turned down the lights so that she would be able to sleep.

"Marcia?"

Her voice sounded far away, as if it were coming from beneath a cotton wall. Thinking of cotton made her realize that her mouth had gotten dry, and she tried to lick her lips.

The dripping was even louder now, until it was a roar within her head. What was it? And what was the whooshing that underlay it?

Lucille felt suddenly cold. The tingling in her hands was spreading through her body. What on earth was happening to her?

Maybe she should get up, break an ammonia ampule, and inhale the vapors. That would get the blood back to her head. Yes. She should do that.

But when she tried to move, her arms and legs were

leaden. It was all she could do to raise her head a few inches off the table.

She blinked and squinted and saw what the source of the dripping was: the tubing running from her arm to the collection bag had been severed. The bag wasn't even a quarter full.

Her blood was dripping from the tubing onto the floor. Her blood was making that sound.

The puddle of her blood was spreading rapidly. There was a lot more blood on the floor than in the bag. A lot more.

Even in the fog of her confusion, she felt a momentary surprise at how fast the blood was dripping. She was, what did they call it? Exsanguinating . . .

Bleeding to death . . .

If she could scream, she would have.

Instead, she laid her head down, licked her lips again, and closed her eyes.

If only she could loosen the tourniquet around her arm. If only she could pull the needle out of her vein. If only someone would come.

If only the dripping would stop . . .

Twenty-Eight

Bronwyn lay still, her eyes closed, breathing evenly through her mouth, pretending to be asleep.

Samantha stood at the bedside watching her for what seemed like the longest time. Finally, she reached and straightened the blanket, then turned and quietly left the room.

In the sliver of light coming through the open door Bronwyn could see the clock.

It was nearly midnight.

She had woken over an hour ago to escape another nightmare, but this time she must not have cried out. Instead she had lain, shivering with the cold of it, huddled beneath the covers, more frightened than she'd ever been in her life.

This time, though, there hadn't been a figure, only the voice.

Bronwyn, it had said.

Again she'd felt the tingling, the cold pressing in on her as if it were alive, the numbness that covered her face like a mask.

Bronwyn Grace.

The voice whispered in her mind, sending tentacles of icy sound through her body until her very being

217

quivered from it.

You are my child.

She knew it was her mother who had called her from her sleep. It was her mother's voice that whispered to her. She was sure of that, although she'd never heard the voice until now.

My child.

That dreadful cold engulfed her, spiders of ice dancing on her face, and she saw a spear of brilliant blue light as it entered her right eye. It hurt less than it had before, as though a barrier had been broken down, as though a path had been cleared for it.

Bronwyn, the voice rasped, *do you know how long I have waited for you?*

This time, the blood came from her nose, running warm across her frozen face.

Bronwyn, you are my child.

She had no idea how long the nightmare lasted, how long the blue light had filled her head, but when it was over, she was very tired and her head ached. Even so, she had gotten up, and working silently, had stripped the blood-stained sheets from her bed.

After a moment's thought, she stuffed them under the bed, where the ruffle would hide them from view.

The clean sheets were stored on the top shelf in her closet, and she opened the door an inch at a time, so that the hinges wouldn't squeak. When there was enough room for her to fit through, she stepped inside. She hadn't a footstool so she pulled out the lowest of the built-in drawers and stepped on it, using the added height to get a knee up onto one of the lower sweater shelves, and then pulling herself up.

Standing upright on that shelf, she could barely

reach the sheets, but she managed to grab the corner of one and she yanked it free of the stack. The other sheets tumbled to the floor.

Bronwyn got down in reverse order of how she'd gotten up, and kneeled on the floor, cramming the extra sheets into the open drawer, which she pushed shut.

She had helped Mrs. Henderson make the bed many times, and didn't remember it taking very long, but in the near dark she started to put the top sheet on sideways, and had to start over again.

All the while she was waiting for the door to open wider and the light to snap on.

If Sam or her father asked why she was making the bed in the middle of the night, she would have no explanation to give. She wasn't really sure herself, except it seemed important that no one know about the blood.

Finally, she was done, and she got back into bed. A scant minute later, Sam came to the door.

Now, lying wide awake in the darkness, Bronwyn didn't know what to do.

If she told her father what had happened to her, last night in the hospital and tonight in her own bed, would he believe her?

She was old enough to know that only crazy people heard voices that weren't there. Would he, if she told him, think her crazy? Would he send her away?

The thought of it made her squirm.

When she was in first grade, the mother of one of her classmates had been taken to a special hospital after she'd stopped in the middle of a street, grabbed her head with both hands, and started screaming and laughing at the same time.

An older boy at school, who'd heard his parents talking, informed the group of children gathered around him that it took three grown men to subdue her—Bronwyn had looked the word up later—and that she'd been carted off in an ambulance that same day.

As far as Bronwyn knew, the woman was still wherever they'd taken her.

Maybe hearing voices wasn't as bad as acting crazy in the streets, but she didn't want to do anything that might get her "taken away."

All she knew for sure was that something terrible was going on, and it wasn't normal.

Worst of all, it had to do with her mother.

How could she tell *anyone* that?

Sunday

Twenty-Nine

June 17th

Percy Smitson sat at his desk and watched bleary-eyed as the sun came up.

The clouds that everyone had been expecting had finally arrived, but they were scattered, and the sunlight filtered through.

If he hadn't spent the night there, he might have found the morning sky beautiful, a palette of blue, pink, and gold, the clouds swept along by the wind.

As it was, he would have been satisfied to remain in the cover of darkness. Morning brought trouble, as sure as the sun had risen.

There had been another one last night.

As of now, he had three inexplicable deaths on his hands. What was the old superstition, that death came in threes?

If only he could be sure it would stop at three; he had a sneaking suspicion it wouldn't.

He also had a morgue that was past its capacity, although—thank God—four of the seven bodies were from the accident yesterday.

He had police sniffing around, asking questions

and hinting that they might file murder charges against Viola even though the man was clearly incompetent to chew his food, much less form intent.

He had investigators from the state due to arrive on Monday with the clipboards and regulations and pinched mouths.

And he had a staff that was growing increasingly more nervous.

Not that he blamed them; something very strange was going on. Whatever was at the heart of it, it wasn't the kind of thing they taught MBAs to handle. He hadn't taken a course in Spooky 101.

Nothing in his experience prepared him for catatonic patients attacking doctors or machines electrocuting janitors or lab techs bleeding to death.

He'd been called to the lab after that incident, and it was one of the few times he'd ever felt near fainting. He would never have believed how much blood there'd been if he hadn't seen it with his own eyes. The pool of blood had seemed as big as a lake.

And even all these hours later, he was still shocked at how ghastly pale a bloodless corpse could be. She'd looked as if she'd been carved from wax.

One of the odder things about that particular death was the discovery of a pair of bandage scissors in the dead woman's hand. Lab techs as a rule didn't carry scissors, and no one had a clue as to where they might have come from, but the implication was that she had for some reason cut the tubing and brought about her own death.

Percy sighed and rubbed at his forehead, trying to massage away the ache in his brain.

What he needed now was a way to cover his ass on all fronts.

To that end, he'd used a master key to get into the biomedical engineer's private office, and had recovered the memo he'd sent okaying a delay in equipment testing. He had found the other copies of the memo—the green in his files, the pink in his secretary's—and had destroyed all three, first putting them through the paper shredder and then burning the remains.

With the memo safely disposed of, he felt on solid ground as far as liability for the first death, and after all, the man had merely been a janitor. His passing could hardly be considered a loss to mankind.

In Dr. Armstrong's case, neither his position nor his course of action was as clear.

He'd phoned an attorney friend in Sacramento to get a legal reading of the lay of the land, and had been advised that a great deal would depend on whether the hospital could be considered negligent for not having restrained Mr. Viola to keep him from harming himself or others. In other words, the hospital might be at fault.

However, if Mr. Viola's doctor had deemed his patient not in need of restraint, the liability, or most of it, would be the doctor's. Or, given the patient's history, possibly the criminal justice system which had dumped him on Point Hansen Hospital rather than keeping him under lock and key might be culpable.

Percy didn't care one way or the other, as long as *he* was held blameless.

As for the lab tech, he was fully prepared to swear on a stack of Bibles that he believed she harbored suicidal tendencies. He would write a confidential personnel report—and back-date it—suggesting that she be offered counseling to deal with her recent bout of depression.

No doubt there were co-workers or friends who would dispute that, but it would be their word against his. And how would they explain the scissors?

The best outcome would include a police finding that her fingerprints were the only ones on the scissors, and that the scissors had indeed cut the tubing.

He would keep his fingers crossed, figuratively speaking, that that would prove to be the case. And if he got off scot-free on all counts, he would celebrate his good fortune by getting rip-roaring drunk.

Percy waited until seven-thirty A.M., and when his phone hadn't rung with reports that the day-shift staff was too skittish to work and were abandoning ship, he decided it was safe to go on home.

He had just put on his jacket when someone knocked on the door.

He turned and saw the person he least wanted to see after a sleepless night. "Wyatt, you're up and at 'em early this morning."

"I need to talk to you."

Percy motioned to the chair opposite his desk. "What's on your mind?"

English ignored the invitation to sit down, and remained standing. "The trauma unit."

Percy smiled, hoping his irritation didn't show. "You'll have to be a little more patient. I haven't had time to set up a board meeting to discuss it, but I'll get to it first thing tomorrow morning."

"Don't bother."

"Excuse me?"

"I called them myself."

"You . . . called the board members?" Percy didn't like this at all.

English nodded. "I called each and every one of them, and explained what had happened yesterday— the head-on collision, the number of victims, the

226

severity of their injuries—and suggested that we could have saved at least one and possibly two of the four who died."

"Well," Percy said, sitting in his chair, leaning back and steepling his hands on his chest, "you know I would never presume to question your medical judgment, but I'm not sure that I agree with that. The young man who had the aneurysm . . . from what I heard, I don't think anyone could have saved him."

"If we had a fully equipped trauma unit, and more importantly, the trained staff to provide care, we could have had him into surgery in minutes, not hours."

"Ah yes, surgery." The panacea of the truly desperate.

"By the time we located a surgeon to come in, it was most likely already too late. If we have a dedicated trauma unit, we'll be able to keep a surgical team ready twenty-four hours a day."

"Yes, well, *a* surgical team. But tell me, wouldn't the girl you admitted have benefited from surgery too? What did she die of?"

"Head injuries and a lacerated liver."

"So . . . which one would you save? Hmm? Because even if we somehow managed to afford this trauma unit with all its bells and whistles, there is a limit involved. You might have saved one of those young people, maybe, but then, maybe not."

"Damn it, we have to try."

"Damn it, you can't save everyone!" Percy realized he was yelling and lowered his voice. "The problem is, Wyatt, you don't want to accept that people are going to die and there's nothing you doctors can do about it."

"We can—"

"No. Pardon me for telling the truth, but there are people whose lives you couldn't save if you had every surgeon, every nurse, every piece of medical equipment that was ever made. Some people are going to die, period. End of story." Percy got up abruptly. "Doctors are not gods. *You can't save everyone.*"

"I never said we could."

"You never said it, but you think it." He tapped the side of his head with his index finger. "In your brain, you believe it. Every time someone saves a life that five years ago would have been unsalvageable, it gives you ideas. No matter that you bankrupt the system."

The expression on English's face had darkened. "It's better, in your opinion, to let them all die, rather than spend the money. Why? Is there no return on saving human lives?"

Percy knew this was thin ice to be treading on, but he was so damned tired of the same bleeding-heart arguments. He said, "Is there a return? What have you gotten in return from your wife being saved?"

"You—"

"It costs in excess of two hundred thousand dollars a year to keep her alive. Two hundred thousand dollars. And from the very first day there was no hope that she'd ever recover."

English remained silent, almost ominously so, and if he weren't so tired, Percy would have stopped at that and left the rest unsaid.

But he didn't. "She is using up valuable resources, *scarce* resources, taking up hours of skilled nursing care, and for what?"

"For what?" English repeated.

"Is she ever going to walk out of here? Is she ever going to repay the system that provides for her? Oh, sure, your insurance covers most of the cost, but who is paying for it, really?"

"That's not your concern."

"It is my concern, and everyone's concern. What is your wife's life worth? Is it worth a million dollars? A million and a half? Look at what's on the meter, man. The ride is over, and what do you have to show for it?"

English's voice was so quiet that he could barely hear him. "I doubt that you, with your bottom line and systems, could ever hope to understand."

"It's you who don't get it, Wyatt. The best thing you ever could have done for your wife was pull the plug. It was never economically feasible to keep her alive." Percy squinted, concentrating hard. "How many of those people you were so anxious to save do you think died because *she* ate up their share of the medical pie?"

For a second, seeing the rage in the other man's eyes, he thought that he'd gone too far, that English was going to haul off and hit him. Instead, the doctor headed for the door.

Percy felt a thrill of victory.

At the door, Wyatt English stopped and turned to face him. "What I came here to tell you was that the Board has unanimously agreed to support a trauma unit. The decision has been made."

"I'll have to go on record as opposing it," Smitson said, lifting his chin.

"You might want to reconsider."

There was something in English's tone that bothered him, triggering a warning signal in the back of his mind, but he ignored it. "There's nothing to reconsider."

"I see. Then I have no choice but to accept your resignation."

"My . . . I'm not resigning."

"I advise that you do."

"Is that a threat?"

"Not at all. It's important that the hospital's administrator be enthusiastic and supportive of the new direction we're taking, and if you can't be, then it's best that we part company."

"You can't do this," Percy said.

"It's strictly a management decision, surely you understand that. And in the long run, we both know it's better for you to resign than to have another dismissal on your record."

"The Board isn't going to appreciate your making a decision of this magnitude without consulting them."

"I did consult them. They approved it. As a matter of fact, more than one board member wanted to know why we hadn't made the change before now."

That knocked the legs out from under him, and he sat down heavily in his chair. "What?"

"It hasn't gone unnoticed that your administrative style is a bit corrosive. We've received several complaints from employees, and even one or two from patients."

"I don't . . ."

"You can't treat people like numbers in a column, Percy. That's the bottom line of *this* system."

Thirty

The phone rang.

Cassie Owens raised her head off the pillow, looked at the clock, and groaned. A quarter to eight? Who in the world would be calling her at a quarter to eight on a Sunday morning?

She wanted to rip the phone out of the wall and fling it through the window. She wanted it to land in the street where a steam roller would flatten it, backing over it once or twice and crushing it into a billion little intrusive pieces.

And then she'd send the steam roller after whoever was on the other end.

She considered covering her head with the pillow and trying to ignore the ringing, but she was awake now, so Cassie reached out grudgingly and picked up the receiver. "Hello?"

"Cassie, it's Barbara at the hospital."

Barbara Sullivan was the supervisor of nurses. Cassie covered her eyes with her hand, shielding out the morning light. "Yes?"

"I was wondering if you'd be willing to come in this morning."

"This morning?"

231

"I know you worked a P.M. shift last night, and under normal circumstances I wouldn't ask you to double-back and cover a day shift—"

"But?"

"But, as it is, we're extremely shorthanded this morning, and we could really use a few warm . . . we could really use the help."

Warm bodies, Cassie thought, that's what she was going to say. She smiled grimly. "I don't know, I've only had a few hours of sleep." In fact, she'd stayed up watching an old Humphrey Bogart movie until five A.M.

"You'll get time and a half for the shift, if that's any incentive."

It was and then again it wasn't. She rose up on one elbow and ran a hand through her hair. "What floor would I be working?"

"Well, it would be West."

"Shit, Barbara, you know how much I hate working West. And bad as it is in the evenings, it's ten times worse on the day shift."

"I know, but—"

"Sorry, I can tell you're in a bind, and I'd really like to help you out." Cassie was lying through her teeth. "Maybe some other time. Okay?"

"Listen," Barbara said quickly, "there's nothing I can do about today's shift, but if you do come in, I'll take you off West for Monday and Tuesday."

Cassie hesitated. This definitely was a bargaining chip she could use to her advantage. "How about taking me off West entirely?"

"I'm not sure I can do that, Cassie. All of us have to work shifts and wings we're not happy with once in a while. The reality is, I need to cover all the floors twenty-four hours a day, seven days a week, fifty-two weeks a year."

"There are nurses who have never worked West," Cassie said pointedly.

"Yes, but they've got years of seniority. Rank does have some privileges."

Cassie said nothing. Her best move was to stay silent. She heard static on the line and then the sound of papers being shuffled.

Come on.

"I could clear you from that rotation for the next six months," the supervisor of nurses said.

Cassie was tempted to hold out for more, a year perhaps, but there was a possibility that Barbara would say no, and find someone else willing to work today, with no strings attached. Then she'd be facing two more days on West and who knew what else in the months to come?

"All right," she said. "I'll do it."

"Good."

"I'll be there in thirty minutes or so," Cassie said, and hung up the phone. "Hallelujah! My last shift on West for six months."

She got out of bed and headed into the bathroom to start getting ready.

It was sprinkling when she stepped outside, and Cassie hurried to her car.

One day more on West, and a short one at that. She'd punch in around eight-thirty and get off at half-past three. Minus thirty minutes for lunch, it came to six and a half hours.

Six and a half hours of The Zombie Ward. She could handle that.

She grinned at her own reflection in the rearview mirror, recalling the supervisor's near slip about warm bodies. If that was really all they needed, they

233

could prop up a few of the coma patients in chairs at the nurse's stations and save themselves from having to pay a lot of overtime.

The rain was coming down fairly hard by the time she arrived at the hospital. She dug around in the glove compartment and found an old fold-up plastic rain bonnet that she'd gotten free from her insurance agent.

She made it into the building without getting too wet, wadded the rain bonnet up and shoved it in her uniform pocket, and headed for the time clock.

There, on the schedule, was confirmation of her deal: the *W*'s had been erased and *N*'s had been written in. North was the medical wing. Twenty-five beds, she'd be assigned five patients maximum, none of whom would be among the living dead.

Cassie kissed her fingertips and held them to those precious *N*'s.

Six and a half hours, and I'll be free.

"What are you so happy about?" the day-shift unit secretary asked.

Cassie merely smiled. She had finished taking an abbreviated version of report from the floor-charge nurse and was copying down details of the nursing care she would be providing her patients.

"Have you heard about all the weird things going on around here?" The secretary looked apprehensive. "People dying and all that?"

"I heard," Cassie said. "I have a philosophy about death . . . when your number's up, you die."

"Well, that's certainly cheering."

She shrugged. "What it is, is cheeringly certain. Face it, we're all going to die, sooner or later."

"If it's all the same to you," the secretary said

234

reaching for the ringing phone, "I'll die later. I just paid off my Visa account, and I want to go owing a lot of money. A *lot* of it."

She started with Rath in 8-West, deciding to get the most physically demanding of her three patients over with first.

Thelma Rath was in a cocktail coma, her loss of consciousness resulting from a rather imprudent and substantial mixing of alcohol and Valium. She was in her sixties, and was a huge woman whose wasting away would never occur in the time she had left to live.

Because of her size, every aspect of her care was more complicated. To shift her position in bed required a system of belts and pulleys, which were routed over a metal overhead bar that extended the length of the bed, then hooked up to a hand crank.

Giving her a bath took the better part of an hour, what with all the folds of skin that had to be cleaned and powdered to guard against chafing. Her patient gowns had to be specially made.

And instead of the nasogastric tube used to feed most of the coma patients, Big Thelma had a slightly larger tube which had been surgically implanted in her stomach. Twice it had become infected, and her doctors were considering trying hyperalimentation.

In hyperalimentation, a hypertonic solution—glucose, vitamins, amino acids, and electrolytes—would be infused intravenously, the doctor would thread a catheter through the subclavian vein and into the superior vena cava which empties into the right atrium of the heart. The solution would thus be diluted by the large volume of blood passing through the heart.

It wasn't a procedure they used often, and was generally reserved for only the most critically ill patients. Rath qualified on that count.

Even as a nurse, Cassie found the concept of hyperalimentation gruesome and disquieting. The image she could never quite clear from her mind was that they were feeding the heart.

A friend in nursing school had joked about patients with hungry hearts, but Cassie hadn't laughed then, and she wasn't laughing now.

At least, she thought, if they go ahead with it, I won't be around. And with any luck, during the six-month sabbatical from West that Cassie had coming, Big Thelma would succumb to one of the other fates that so often befell the obese patients.

"I hope your number comes up before Christmas," she said. "Because I want to have a happy New Year."

After Rath, caring for her other two patients was relatively easy.

Cassie noted that, free of all of her restraints and braces, Deborah English had begun to tighten up, her arms tucking inward as though she wanted to hug herself. Her legs had also begun to draw up to her chest; if she survived much longer, she would no doubt at last achieve the fetal position common to coma patients that physical therapy had denied her all these years.

Her temperature had spiked again, and was up to one hundred and four point six.

Curiously, though, she felt cool to the touch, almost cold.

Cassie gave her a quick sponge bath, washed her hair, changed the linens on the bed, and dressed her in a clean gown. She noticed that there were crystals in the urinary catheter line but decided against mentioning it in her progress notes. At this point in the game, what harm would a urinary-tract infection do?

Maybe the urinary infection would hasten the process of dying.

She was just finishing when she heard someone enter the room behind her and turned to see Wyatt English. As usual, he seemed only to have eyes for his wife. He crossed directly to her bedside.

"Dr. English," Cassie said.

"How is she?" he asked without looking up.

A part of her was afraid to tell him the truth, but she had more to fear from lying. "Not well, I'm sorry to say. Her temp is up, and I think her respirations are becoming increasingly labored."

He touched the back of his hand to Deborah's face and stroked her cheek gently.

Cassie looked away.

"It's not long now," he said.

She opened her mouth to agree when it occurred to her that he wasn't talking to her. Something stirred in her at the realization that Wyatt English was offering comfort to his wife, who couldn't hear him and, in any case, was way beyond caring either way.

Cassie felt like an intruder. She left the room, leaving them alone.

When she came back from her lunch break, she was surprised to hear that Mr. Viola had died.

No one had been expecting it, least of all his doctor, since with the exception of his catatonia, he appeared to have been in good health.

His nurse had gone in to spoon-feed him his lunch and had found him in the early stages of rigor mortis.

CPR was thoroughly out of the question.

"Jeez," the secretary said, "they're dropping like flies around here."

Viola's nurse looked up from her paperwork. "What's worse, they're going to have to start stacking the bodies like cordwood."

Cassie laughed and then covered her mouth. "Sorry. It just struck me funny."

That earned her a cold stare. "If you think it's funny, you can take the body down to the morgue."

She had to fight to keep from laughing again. "Sure, I'll do it." It'd waste a few minutes, and if nothing else, she was curious about the eternal sleeping arrangements, as it were. "Is he ready to go?"

The other nurse nodded. "He's all yours."

Cassie wheeled the body along the corridor toward the morgue.

Viola had died in a sitting—or slouching— position, so he'd been placed on the gurney on his side. Covered by a sheet, his form appeared somewhat insectile, and not at all human.

When she turned a corner, the body shifted, and in spite of herself, Cassie jumped.

The halls between West and the morgue were fairly dark under normal conditions, but on Sundays the hospital saved electricity by turning off most of the lights in nonpatient areas. In the dimness, the white sheet became even more of a focal point than usual.

Cassie found herself glancing over her shoulder every few seconds to avoid looking at the body, or maybe, she admitted, to see if anyone was following her. But the hall was deserted.

Even the intercom was silent; she hadn't heard a

page since she'd left West.

The whole thing was giving her the creeps.

Ahead she could see the unmarked door to the morgue. A small light was recessed into the ceiling above it, and it cast a halo of light on the threshold.

A tingle ran the length of her spine and made the hair stand up on her arms.

"Coward," she chastised herself, and laughed, a little nervously. It wasn't as though she'd never been around dead bodies before.

Some of her best friends were dead bodies.

At the door, she stopped and dug in her pocket, bringing out both the rain bonnet and the key to the morgue. She put the bonnet on the gurney, inserted the key, and twisted the doorknob.

Inside, she had to prop the door open with a waste basket. Then she pulled Mr. Viola headfirst into the small room.

One of the gurney's rear wheels wobbled and a corner of the damned thing hit the door. The waste basket tipped over and rolled a few feet, which allowed the door to swing closed. The door was heavy, and Cassie heard a loud click as the lock engaged.

"Shit," she said.

Well, she had the key.

The morgue *was* full.

There were gurneys beside each one of the refrigerated drawers, and on the gurneys were the extra bodies, covered by sheets. One of the bodies was quite small, and it had been wrapped rather than just covered.

Another of the bodies had a hand showing from beneath the sheet. A male hand, and kind of swollen, its fingers were skinned across the knuckles. The sheet was stained with a fine spray of dried blood.

Cassie grimaced. They could at least make sure the sheets were clean, she thought.

It took some maneuvering, but she finally managed to work Mr. Viola in between two of the other gurneys. If one more person died today, they'd either have to start stacking or stand them in the corner.

Hadn't someone said they were going to start the autopsies today?

"Well," she said, taking a deep breath and glancing at her watch, "it's not my problem. I've got three more hours and I'm out of here."

She started for the door and then remembered her rain bonnet. It was a cheap throwaway thing, worth fifty cents if that, but if it was still raining, it would be better than nothing.

Cassie went back for the rain bonnet. Naturally, it was on the far side of the gurney, and she had to reach over Mr. Viola's back to get it.

Fingers, cold and stiff and impossibly strong, closed around her wrist.

"Ahh."

The form beneath the sheet began to twist and turn, writhing, each jerky move accompanied by a dreadful ripping sound.

Cassie's mouth went dry and her heart pounded furiously as she tried to pull her wrist from the dead man's powerful grasp. She watched breathlessly as his second hand began to pull the sheet down.

The top of the head was now visible, the skin gray and mottled, with flakes of dead skin here and there. His hair had been thinning on top and the long strands someone had combed to cover his bald pate were standing upright, in a parody of fright.

"Oh God, oh no, oh no," she whimpered.

240

Wait, he must be still alive. That's it, he's waking up and he's frightened and that's why he's holding on so tight. God, let that be it.

But when his face was fully exposed, his features were contorted and frozen in the rictus of death. His eyelids were open, but his eyes had rolled back and only the bloodshot whites were visible.

Cassie screamed.

He lurched up and put his free hand on the back of her head, pulling her toward him until their faces were inches apart. Slowly, inexorably, his mouth neared hers, and he gave her the kiss of death, sucking the air right out of her lungs.

Her heartbeat stopped before she fell to the floor.

Thirty-One

Barbara Sullivan locked the nursing office and set off on her rounds.

It was her practice to visit every nurse's station at some point during the shift, usually in late morning. Today, however, the staffing crisis had kept her fully occupied until now.

It was nearly two o'clock; the evening shift would be arriving before long.

She decided to start in ICU which shared a wing with South, then check in on West, North, and finish on Maternity in the east wing which would bring her full circle and back within the vicinity of her office.

At three, she'd give report to the P.M. supervisor, and then she was going to go home, take a hot bath, drink an Irish coffee, and try to forget about this day.

The nurses' attitudes about recent events had caught her off guard. She never would have expected a case of the white flu—nurses calling in sick because they were unwilling to come to work—as a result of the unfortunate coincidences of the past few days.

Perhaps it was naive of her, but she'd thought she could reason with them, and make them see that their fears were groundless. She'd talked herself hoarse and had very little to show for it.

A few of the nurses had even gone so far as to suggest that there was a murderer on the hospital grounds. As though Point Hansen Hospital were harboring a supernatural fiend, as in all those teenage slasher movies.

She'd had to bite her tongue to keep from telling those nurses to grow up.

One had suggested that the killer was Mr. Viola, who after all had been caught in the act once. She insinuated that his catatonic state was a put-on, and that when the opportunity arose, he slipped from his room and went out hunting for victims.

Of course, now Mr. Viola had died—of natural causes, Barbara was sure—so if he *had* been the killer, that particular nurse should consider herself safe.

Unless he was one of those indestructible supernatural fiends, that is.

Barbara chuckled softly, amused.

Personally, she was certain that when all was said and done, there would be a reasonable explanation for the deaths. Her job was to try to keep things under control until it all blew over.

ICU was quiet, for a change. The patients were not as restive as they'd been yesterday, and the nurses, thankful for the respite, were catching up on the mountain of paperwork that accumulated hourly.

It took less than five minutes to get a brief report on the patients, and she arranged with one nurse to work two hours of overtime to cover one of the evening crew who was attending a wedding that afternoon.

Barbara went on to the surgical floor, where they were quite busy with new admits. Monday was the preferred day for elective surgery. and they usually

244

had a full house. The good part was these patients were not demanding and their care wasn't time consuming.

After their operations it would be a different story; then they'd have aches and pains and complaints, real or imagined.

She signed off ten milligrams of injectable Valium that a nurse had wasted, making a mental note to beware if it happened again. Drug abuse among nurses was far too common to overlook the possibility that someone had used the drug on herself and only claimed to have "lost" it.

The more frequent occurrence was for the nurse to give the patient for whom the drug was ordered an injection of sterile water, and keep the real stuff secreted away for later use.

"Anything else?" she asked the surgical charge nurse as she was ready to leave.

"Make it three-thirty," the charge nurse replied.

"If I could, I would. You're not the only one who'll be glad when this day is over."

On West she found a tempest brewing.

"She always does things like that," one of the nurses said as Barbara neared the station. "I don't see how they stand her on the evening shift."

"I know what you mean. If *I* had to work with her all the time, I'd sit that miss down and give her a talking-to she wouldn't soon forget."

"What's going on?" Barbara asked, knowing she'd probably regret it.

"Owens. She offered to take Viola to the morgue and she isn't back yet."

"When was this?"

The nurses exchanged looks. "I don't know, after

245

lunch sometime."

"What time did she take her break?" Lunches were spread over a two-hour block, so it could be anywhere from eleven-thirty to one-thirty.

"She was on a break from the moment she got here," one nurse said.

The second added: "I know she went on her break before I had mine, so she's been gone a couple of hours, at the least."

The secretary shook her head. "It hasn't been *that* long. She did take an early lunch and was back at twelve, but I don't think she left with the . . . with Mr. Viola until one."

"That would still make it an hour and a half that she's been gone," the second nurse said. "It doesn't take an hour and a half to deliver a body."

Barbara frowned. "Has anyone checked to see whether she made it to the morgue or not?"

"No."

She set her clipboard on the counter. "I'd better take a look."

She jingled her keys in her lab-coat pocket as she walked down the darkened hallway toward the morgue. She stopped at a ladies' restroom to see if perhaps Cassie was inside, thinking maybe she'd taken sick on the way back from the morgue. It had been known to happen; nurses weren't entirely immune to the special sights and smells of the autopsy room.

Her footsteps echoed on the tile floor. She checked all of the stalls, but the place was empty.

Turning, she caught a glimpse of her reflection in the mirror and the sudden movement made her start. She laughed at her own foolishness; for one brief moment she'd believed it was the killer. . . .

She was a little old to be the heroine, cornered and facing death.

At the morgue, she took out her key ring, picking through them until she found the correct one. She noticed as she unlocked the door that there was light showing at the foot of it.

"Cassie?" she said.

Her eyes went first to the spectacle of Mr. Viola in all his naked glory and then, reluctantly, to Cassie Owens, dead on the floor.

There was not the slightest doubt that she was dead; her face was suffused with color, typical of a certain type of suffocation, and her tongue protruded slightly. Some kind of clear plastic was wrapped around her neck.

"Oh my," Barbara Sullivan said. She saw that the plastic ligature was a rain cap, and thought perversely and entirely inappropriately that she'd forgotten to bring her own.

The police would keep her here for hours over this, and it was sure to be raining harder by the time they let her leave.

Thirty-Two

Even though it was raining, Bronwyn wanted to go to the beach.

Sam wasn't sure it was the best idea she'd ever heard, but finally she agreed, with the provisions that the child dress warmly and, if it began raining harder, she would leave without any argument.

In fact, Samantha loved the beach on rainy days, when it was largely deserted. The tourists stayed away, and the locals had better things to do.

They walked down the street to her house so she could borrow her mother's car. She was thankful that Bronwyn was with her so she didn't have to endure another inquisition or listen to any more gossip.

"Make sure she wears a nice warm cap," her mother said. "Remember, most of the heat escapes the body through the top of the head."

"Yes, Mother," Sam said.

As she backed the car out of the driveway, she noticed her mother at the window, curtain drawn aside, and had to smile at her worried look. She waved and got an answering wave, if a rather tentative one, in return.

Sam didn't understand what her mother had to be

worried about; it wasn't as though she were heading off into the great unknown.

There was only one other car in the gravel lot that served Lighthouse Beach. Its owner was nowhere in sight.

"Well," Sam said, locking the door after Bronwyn, "we've pretty much got the place to ourselves."

They crossed the lot, gravel crunching beneath their feet, and started down the incline toward the beach. The dirt pathway was a little more treacherous than usual because of the rain, but they took their time, and made it safely down.

Bronwyn, when they reached the sand, took off at a run for the water's edge.

Sam followed after her. The rain had become more of a mist, and it and the spray from the windswept waves caressed her face as she neared the shoreline.

The child was standing a few inches back from the reach of the water, her expression rapt as she watched·it begin to retreat. Then she bent down and picked up a nearly perfect shell.

"Look," she said, turning to Sam as she brushed the sand from it.

"I remember when there used to be all kinds of shells on this beach. And sand dollars."

"Sand dollars?"

"Yes." Sam shielded her eyes and gazed out to where the waves were breaking, foaming white and wonderful against the dark gray-green of the sea. "They're these round things, I don't even know how to describe them, but I have some at home that I found when I was your age. I'll show them to you."

"I'd like that."

"Come on," Sam said, holding out her hand, "let's

walk toward the point."

Bronwyn's small hand disappeared in hers, and she smiled up at her. "Thank you for bringing me here," she said. "I've always wanted to come."

Both the smile and the sentiment pleased Sam. "You're more than welcome."

They walked at a leisurely pace, stopping now and then so that Bronwyn could investigate some treasure, another shell, a piece of driftwood, or a bit of colored glass worn smooth by the sea. Before long, the pockets of the child's jeans were full to overflowing and they had to start using Sam's.

"Do you like my father?" Bronwyn asked, from out of the blue.

"Yes I do. He's a very nice man."

Bronwyn nodded. "He is. And he likes you."

At first, Sam didn't know what to say to that, but she realized that Bronwyn was waiting for some kind of response from her. "I'm glad."

"If he asked you, would you marry him?"

If the first question had caught her off guard, the last left her momentarily speechless even though her heart had an answer. Finally, she said, "Your dad is already married, Bronwyn, to your mom."

"I know, but . . . she isn't going to live."

Sam wasn't prepared to have this conversation. She pointed out at the ocean. "Look! Do you see that dark thing in the water? I think it's a seal."

Bronwyn gazed in that direction, but when she turned back, the question was still in her eyes and it was clear that she wouldn't be distracted. "My dad is going to need somebody, when my mom dies."

Where was Benjamin Spock when you needed him? Sam wondered. "He has you," she said, feeling desperately inadequate.

"It's not the same."

251

She couldn't argue that. She cleared her throat. "No, it isn't, but when your mother . . . dies . . . your dad is going to need you more than anyone else."

The words were barely out of her when she wanted to take them back; providing emotional support for her father in the wake of her mother's death was no doubt more of a burden than a kid Bronwyn's age could handle.

"Of course," Sam added, "I'll do whatever I can for both of you when it . . . if she . . ."

Serious eyes looked into hers. "She *is* going to die. Very soon."

Samantha recognized the certainty in her voice and wondered at the source of it. Had she overheard someone talking? If so, it must have been a terrible thing for her to hear. . . .

"My dad doesn't like to let people know how bad he feels," Bronwyn said, "but I know."

Sam saw at once that for all her matter-of-factness, the child was hurting too. She put an arm around her, hugging her close. She kissed the top of her head through the wet wool of her stocking cap.

"You might not think so now, but you will get through whatever happens. And your dad . . . well, I think you'll have to leave it up to him to find the someone he needs when the time comes."

"It could be you as well as anyone," Bronwyn said. "I hope it is."

Was she so transparent that the little girl had picked up on her own feelings? "If it is—and I'm not saying I think it will be or even could be—I'd be very lucky to have both of you."

There was no mistaking the satisfaction in those hazel eyes.

"Good," Bronwyn said, and nodded, as though something had been settled.

They walked on in silence, leaving footprints in the wet sand for the waves to wash away.

The darker clouds that had been hovering off the coast all morning began to move in, and Samantha decided it was time to head back to the car. Bronwyn, as promised, didn't argue.

They were starting up the pathway to the parking lot when it really started coming down, big fat drops of warm rain.

"Hurry," she said.

Bronwyn clambered up the incline with a dancer's grace, her footing sure, her balance perfect. Then she vanished over the top.

"Not that fast," Sam said under her breath, unable to keep up. Her foot slid in a muddy patch and she landed hard on one knee. She regained her feet and continued upward, the rain pelting her, running down the back of her neck, beneath her clothes.

When she reached the top, she looked around for Bronwyn but didn't see her. The other car that had been there earlier was gone.

"Bronwyn?"

She started running, but the unevenness of the gravel hampered her progress. Her ankle turned and she nearly pitched forward onto her face. She skinned her hands catching herself.

"Bronwyn?"

The rain had gotten into her eyes, and it made it difficult to see. She wiped at her face, but her hands were none too clean and that only made it worse.

Then she saw a small form huddled near the car.

The child was sitting, her arms hugging her knees to her chest, her head bent forward and resting on her knees, her face hidden.

Had she hurt herself?

Sam ran, the sound of her own breathing loud in her ears. Overhead there was a flash of light, followed quickly by a thunderclap.

"Great," she said.

When she reached the car she knelt down beside the child, putting one hand on her shoulder. Maybe the strain of climbing after the fall she'd taken on Friday had driven the air from her lungs. "Bronwyn? What is it? Are you all right?"

"Yes," came the muffled reply.

"Honey, come on then, get up and get in the car. You're getting soaked and the storm is getting worse." Another flash of lightning and a booming roll of thunder served as verification.

"Please . . . leave me alone for a minute."

Sam could see that the child was trembling. The legs of her jeans were wet through and they clung to her. The knit ski cap she wore was sodden.

"Bronwyn, what's the matter? Are you feeling sick?" She remembered vaguely from a first-aid class she'd taken her freshman year that one of the symptoms of a concussion was nausea.

"It will pass in a minute."

"Are you dizzy? Let me help you into the car where it's nice and dry." She cast a nervous glance skyward. The clouds seemed to be boiling and churning from some internal source.

"Please, wait."

There was a quality to the little girl's voice Sam had never heard before, almost as if she was warning her to keep away. . . .

Sam ducked her head, trying to see through the concealment of the child's sheltering arms. She touched a small hand and was startled at how cold it was.

254

"You're freezing," she said. "You'll catch your death of cold."

"It's nearly over."

"Bronwyn, you're scaring me. Whatever is wrong, let me help you."

A shudder passed through the child, and she gasped, rocking back and forth as though in pain. Her hands clenched into fists.

Sam was torn over what to do. She could pick the child up bodily and put her in the car, or run to the nearest house and call for help.

But what if Bronwyn was simply crying? Heaven knew she had reason. Wasn't she entitled to her privacy, even in the middle of a thunderstorm?

"Let me help you," she said again, more softly. "Tell me what it is and I'll help you."

Bronwyn slowly began to lift her head, and when Sam saw her face, she thought for one frightening moment that *she* might faint.

The child had been crying, but her tears were tears of blood.

"No one can help me," Bronwyn said.

Sam's heart was hammering so hard she thought that it might burst, but she tried to ignore it. All she wanted to do was get the child safely to the hospital and notify Wyatt of what had happened to her.

Beside her, Bronwyn sat quietly, staring straight ahead without expression.

The tears were gone. She'd found a package of facial tissues in the glove box and wiped the little girl's face. The bloodied tissues were on the seat between them; she would show them to Wyatt so that he would believe her. He had to believe her.

Just get there and worry about that later.

255

There wasn't a lot of traffic on the streets, and she was making good time. She ran one red light, partly because of the way it reflected on the wet pavement. A pool of blood was the last thing she wanted to think about.

When she was in sight of the hospital, she began to breathe easier. The sign for the Emergency Room glowed in the near dark brought by the advancing storm. The windshield wipers beat rhythmically, hypnotically.

Sam glanced sideways at Bronwyn.

"Almost there," she said.

The child didn't answer.

This time she insisted on going back in the treatment room with Bronwyn, unmindful of the nurse's disapproving manner.

"Call Dr. English, and tell him I have his daughter here."

"If you'll tell me what the problem is, the E.R. doctor can take a look at her."

Sam shook her head, feeling stubborn. "I'll tell Dr. English what the problem is, and no one else. Just call him, please."

"Have it your way," the nurse said and shrugged.

"I intend to."

Then they were alone. Sam couldn't be still and she paced back and forth in the confines of the examining room. Bronwyn sat on the bed.

"Your dad will be here in a few minutes," she said, hoping she was right. He'd said he would be at the hospital most of the afternoon, but what if he'd finished early and gone home?

She'd left a note at the house that they'd gone to the beach . . . what if he saw that and went out in search of them? He might drive around for an hour or so looking before returning home.

But wait. He had a pager. Sam sighed in relief. "They'll page him," she said, as if saying it would make it so, "and he'll be right here."

Bronwyn didn't reply. Her lips were tinged blue from the cold and her teeth were chattering.

"What am I thinking? Let's get you out of those wet clothes." Sam opened a few cupboard doors until she found a hospital gown and a blanket. "Change into this."

"I don't want to stay here," Bronwyn said. "I'm not going to stay no matter what anyone says."

"Ssh." She pulled off the child's shoes and peeled the wet socks from her feet. "No one is saying you have to stay. I just don't want you catching cold."

"You don't catch cold from being wet," Bronwyn said, almost dreamily.

"Spoken like a true doctor's daughter." Sam grabbed the cuffs and started to tug at the jeans. As wet as they were, they fit like a second skin.

A second skin with lumps, she amended; the pockets were bulging. She stopped yanking and began to empty the pockets of beach treasures so she could roll the jeans down from the waist.

"I . . . I . . ."

Sam looked at her sharply. Her complexion was deathly pale, and the trembling had begun again. "Hold on, kid, please."

Thirty-Three

Ernie Miller let himself into the Physical Therapy office and turned on the lights. A thick sheaf of therapy orders had been stuffed in the plastic box mounted next to the door, and he brought them inside.

Dropping the orders on the desk, he walked over to the whirlpool and turned it on. The water jets came to life, millions of bubbles rising in a steaming froth.

It would feel great on his aching back. One of the perks of this job—and there weren't many—was being able to use the equipment for his own benefit.

His condominium complex had a Jacuzzi, but on weekends it was standing room only, full of aging Lotharios and the empty-headed females that were their prey. Though the rules posted warned against the dangers of drinking alcohol in the spa, it never failed that someone would bring a bottle of champagne to pass around. Which, inevitably, would be shaken by some beer-bellied bozo and sprayed smack in everyone's face, à la the Superbowl—and every other sporting event known to man.

The females would squeal and protest that their mascara would run, holding up their red-taloned hands, as if inch-long nails offered any protection at all, and the guys would laugh uproariously.

Then one of the "girls" as they called themselves, would move until a jet of water was hitting her just so. She'd roll her eyes in ecstasy and comment to the other girls, something to the effect that who needed men, anyway, when they had Jacuzzis to keep them company. And *they* would laugh maliciously.

Ernie had no use for any of his neighbors in general, but those who frequented the spa, he had no use for in particular.

An odd thing about small towns; the residents considered themselves very much "with it" but sometimes at night it was so quiet, the only thing you could hear was the dropping of IQ points.

Anyway, he wasn't one for the hot-tub scene. It was nicer by far to relax in the privacy and comfort of the old hospital whirlpool.

While the water was heating, Ernie decided to go through the therapy orders and divide them into two piles, one for him and the other for Alice. As a way to make amends for getting her riled on Friday, he decided to put most of the difficult patients' orders in his stack.

Among all of the blue order sheets was a pink one, but he laid it aside until he finished with rest.

The pink forms were discontinuation forms. Someone's therapy was being stopped. While he sorted the blues, he let his mind play at guessing whose it was.

If he had a choice in the matter, it would be that insufferable Major Roger Pierpont, United States Army, Retired.

The Major, as he insisted on being called, had a ruptured disk. The exercise regimen his doctor had ordered wasn't overly strenuous, which unfortunately left more wind in the old windbag.

If Ernie had to hear *one more time* about the Big One, the Real War, the War to End All Wars—although it hadn't—he might up and puke. He didn't really care whether the new Army molly-coddled its men, nor did he want to argue the relative merits of the old Sherman tank and the new "monstrosities" that couldn't ford a river "as deep as a piss-ant can piss."

If the Major's therapy was being canceled, it would be an answer to his prayers.

But it wasn't to be; there among the blues was an order increasing the Major's sessions from three times a week to daily.

"Ha!" Ernie said, and put the requisition into Alice's stack. Making amends had its limits.

When he was through, he picked up the pink sheet and saw that it was for Deborah English.

Now *that* qualified as a surprise. Considering who her husband was, Ernie would have wagered that they'd still be doing range of motion exercises on her as they lowered her coffin into the grave.

Had to be nice and limber and tender for those worms, after all.

Ernie snorted, grabbed the master therapy clip-board and saw that her name, unlike most of the others, had been written in ink. He grabbed a bottle of white-out and began dabbing it out.

Losing English wasn't quite as good as losing the Major would have been, but it wasn't a bad compromise. Her treatments took longer than any-one else's, and had fewer results.

So they kept her from folding up like an umbrella the way a lot of coma patients did, the return didn't

261

seem worth the investment of his time. Alice said she didn't mind doing English, but to be fair, they usually alternated weeks.

He'd just finished his week. Didn't it figure that Alice had been saved from doing hers? Somebody up there didn't like him.

Still, life would be a lot easier with English off the schedule. Even with all their efforts, her joints were stiffening up. It made it very difficult to know how much pressure to apply.

He'd never told anyone, but a few months back he had accidentally broken one of the bones in her hand while exercising her fingers. He had heard it crack and felt it give beneath his thumb.

Her hand had swollen up something fierce, until the skin seemed tight enough to split.

Luckily it had happened on a day when a new admit was being transferred in. There was so much turmoil, no one was paying attention to him, and he falsified the records so that it appeared he'd given therapy much earlier in the day. If they wanted to blame the fracture on him, they'd have to find a way to explain how the nurse had missed discovering it for over three hours.

They named the cause as brittle bones. The version he'd heard had her hand being broken when it got caught in the bed rail while the nurse changed her sheets. What it lacked in logic it made up for in simplicity. And he was off the hook.

When he'd seen the day after how black and blue Deborah English's hand was, he'd felt a twinge of guilt, but when he'd finished doing her leg exercises and was drenched with sweat, he'd considered breaking her other hand.

Well, that was all behind him now.

Ernie smiled, remembering how he'd thought she

was looking at him on Friday.

He must have been more tired than he realized.

When he'd finished the paperwork, he went into the changing room to put on his trunks. He hung up his street clothes neatly on a hanger and then went into the open shower stall to rinse off in cool water before getting into the whirlpool.

He grabbed a towel off the linen shelf and padded barefoot over to the tub. The tub was built aboveground, so he climbed the short ladder and stepped over the side into the warm, steaming water.

"Ah."

This was luxury. He set the jets on high, and water pummeled the sore muscles of his back. He closed his eyes and relaxed, all other concerns fading from his mind.

Ernie draped his arms over the side, so that if he went to sleep—a distinct possibility—he wouldn't slide underwater and drown.

The only sounds were the rush of water and an occasional page over the hospital intercom.

He dozed.

Ernie sat bolt upright so quickly that water splashed in his face and he sputtered.

What the hell was that?

Something had moved over among the Nautilus equipment. That part of the department utilized a different light system than the office, and he hadn't bothered to turn those lights on.

The equipment was shrouded in darkness, and even when he squinted, he could barely make out the shapes.

Something, though, had moved back there.

Something or someone.

That was impossible. There was only one door into the department, and he'd locked it after him. Alice had a key, but she would have greeted him if it were her. The same held for the nursing supervisor, who also had a key.

As for Housekeeping, none of that crew could enter the room quietly if their lives depended on it. They each wore ludicrously huge key rings which jingled and jangled like a cowboy's spurs.

So, whatever was moving hadn't just come in.

The hair on the back of Ernie's neck bristled at that thought.

"Hello?"

Deep in the shadows, something stirred.

Ernie backed up against the far side of the whirlpool; if something was coming at him, he wanted to see it before it reached him. He sank deeper in the water, so that most of his body was hidden and he could just see over the rim of the tub.

"This isn't funny," he said.

It ran through his mind that if anything had laughed at that—say, a bloodcurdling laugh—he would have shot straight up in the air.

Great, now he was scaring himself in addition to being afraid of that *thing* over there.

"I don't"—he cleared his throat—"appreciate you playing games with me."

Again, that shifting darkness. He heard a soft thump.

He wanted to get out of the water, but he was afraid to. Being dripping wet and dressed only in his trunks was only the half of it; as long as he'd been in the whirlpool, his muscles would be relaxed to the equivalent of a bowl of Jell-O.

Absurdly, he thought of those silly slasher movies where the dumb girl went out looking for whatever was making noise. The girl would be dressed in a short nightgown or a T-shirt that didn't quite cover her ass—no underwear—and she would go out into the darkness where a dozen other females had been slaughtered in some horrifying fashion. For a weapon, she'd carry a flashlight if she was really dumb or a knife if she was incredibly dumb, because the knife could be used against her.

Ernie had always thought such scenes were excuses to show some naked flesh, which appealed to the voyeurs in the audience, but now he realized that what the moviemakers had done was make the girl almost painfully vulnerable because she had *no clothes*.

He, in his trunks and bare feet, empathized with that heroine. He'd gladly trade places with her, since that was make-believe and this . . . this was real.

"All right," he said, mustering courage from somewhere, "I'm getting out."

Whatever was in the equipment room fell still.

That scared him even more, but he damn well couldn't stay in the whirlpool until Alice arrived at eight in the morning. He moved toward the ladder, keeping low in the water.

When he reached the side he hesitated, narrowing his eyes and trying to identify the shapes he was seeing, to pick out the familiar from the unexpected. The darkness, however, obscured most of it.

Ernie stood and grabbed the ladder railing, then put one leg over the side. The step was cool to his warmed skin. For a moment, he did nothing more, waiting to see if anything was going to come at him.

When nothing happened, he swung his other leg out and turned so he was standing correctly on the steps. There were only four steps, and then he was on the ground.

The fact that he'd gotten this far reassured him. He reached for the towel and wrapped it around his waist. There, he didn't feel as undressed as he had before. That also made him feel more secure.

If he headed for the door, would he reach it before that thing reached him, assuming it would chase him? And if he reached the hall, what then? None of the departments which surrounded Physical Therapy would be open on a Sunday evening.

The hall would be empty. All the doors would be locked. He would have nowhere to hide if it pursued him. It was at least a couple of hundred yards to the nearest place he might seek shelter. Or help.

Ernie shifted his weight from one foot to the other and in the darkness, something did likewise. His muscles went as limp as cooked spaghetti.

Maybe if he tried to reason with it.

"Listen, I don't know what you're doing in here but I'm going to go now. I'll leave you to whatever it is. Okay? If you want money, my wallet is in my pants and they're hanging up in the changing room." He pointed in that direction, in case it didn't know what a changing room was. "Okay, now, I'm leaving."

And the light in the equipment room turned on.

His heart nearly came up his throat and out his mouth. He felt something wet running down the inside of his leg.

There was nothing in the equipment room but equipment. With the light on he could see that there was nothing else there.

"Oh boy," he said, feeling like a fool. What if he'd really gone running down the hall like this. Running and screaming, because he surely would have done both. How would he ever show his face in public again?

He wanted to laugh at his own silliness, but his insides hadn't yet caught up with his brain. Even his smile felt a bit wobbly.

Ernie unwrapped the towel and used it to dry off his legs, then dropped it to the floor to soak up the puddle that had formed. Most of the puddle was water, but not all.

He walked toward the equipment room, willing his thigh muscles to move and his knees not to shake.

Definitely, there was no monster there.

He saw then what had moved; one of the counterbalances on the machine they used to work the trapezius, and anterior, medius, and exterior scalenus muscles—neck muscles—had somehow gotten out of whack and was moving up and down on its own.

Ernie went and stood in front of it, watching as it made two slow repetitions.

"Shit," he said. He sat on the padded bench and got into the correct position, fitting his head into the cushioned metal brace. The machine moved his head up and down, working those muscles and a few others.

Wonderful. He had a machine that . . . that . . . that . . .

Ernie grabbed hold of the brace which seemed to be closing around his face, the sides bending in as though the metal were softening.

"What the . . . ?"

It tightened around his skull, forming itself to the shape of his head and pressing tight until the cushioning was no longer a cushion at all.

Edges of metal bit into his face, and he felt a gush of blood erupt.

It spattered on the floor.

Then the brace started to stretch his neck, which wasn't what it was designed for, but what difference did that make because it was killing him.

Ernie tried to yell, to scream, to cry, but the brace had closed around his face and he couldn't move his jaw, couldn't see, couldn't breathe.

He heard, though, the pop as the vertebrae in his neck were drawn apart, and then his brain filled with red and it was over.

Thirty-Four

"Where is she?" Wyatt asked when he arrived in the Emergency Room.

"Treatment Room Two," the nurse said. "I don't have a chart on her . . . the young lady who brought her in refused to answer any questions."

"Oh? Well, it doesn't matter." He started toward T-2, grabbing a spare stethoscope off a counter.

When he parted the curtain, Samantha turned, her expression dismayed. He couldn't see Bronwyn, but assumed it was she under the blanket.

"It's happening again," Sam said.

"What is?"

"Bronwyn is having some kind of . . . spell, I'd guess you'd call it."

Wyatt stepped up to the bed and felt a momentary shock at seeing his daughter's deathly pale face. Her eyes were closed and she was shivering, but that wasn't what caught his attention: there was bright red blood draining from her right ear.

"What did this?" he asked, thinking she'd ruptured her eardrum in some way. He went to the head of the bed and got an otoscope from the ENT tray.

"Nothing did it, it just happened."

He glanced from Bronwyn to Sam and back again. He could see that her breathing was shallow. "How long ago did it start?"

"A few minutes."

Gently, he turned the child's head to the left and inserted the tip of the otoscope in the ear canal. He did not see the cause of the bleeding, but it was definitely coming from behind the membrane which was bulging. As carefully as he looked, he was unable to detect the hole in the membrane.

He straightened, and tossed the otoscope back on the tray.

Samantha was watching him, her eyes wide with alarm. "Is this from the fall she took?"

"I don't think so." He placed his fingers on Bronwyn's wrist to check her pulse. "She's as cold as ice."

"I know." She sounded miserable. "I took her to the beach—"

"In the rain?"

"I'm sorry. She wanted to go, and she said she'd never been. I thought I'd make it up to her for . . . for what happened on Friday."

"I'm not blaming you, Sam," Wyatt said. It was news to him that Bronwyn had never been to the beach. "But tell me what happened."

"I wish I knew. We went and walked by the water, and she found all these things. . . ."

She gestured toward the foot of the bed, and he saw a collection of shells and stones and blue and green pieces of smoothed glass.

"Everything was fine till we got back to the car. She was sitting on the ground there, bunched up, and she wouldn't let me see her face. I thought first that she was sick to her stomach and then that maybe she was crying, but when she looked up . . . there were bloody tears coming from her eyes."

"Are you saying—"

"She was bleeding from her eyes. I drove her straight here, and I was helping her get undressed, when it started happening again. Only this time, the blood was—"

"Coming from her ears," he finished for her. He looked down at his daughter's face. There were, he saw with some astonishment, tiny clots of blood in the tear ducts. "What the hell is going on?"

"I don't know." Samantha was hugging herself, clearly upset.

He knew of no medical cause for either of the occurrences she'd described. Some kind of stigmata? He shook his head, feeling as confused as Sam looked.

"Did she say anything about what was happening to her?" he asked.

"Only that it had happened before."

"And she didn't tell anyone." He studied the small, wan face.

"No. I think she was afraid she'd have to come back to the hospital."

It was plausible. He moved to the head of the bed again, to get a blood-pressure cuff. He found the small child-sized cuff in an upper cabinet, and attached it.

When he returned to Bronwyn's side, he saw that she was stirring. He put the cuff down and used both hands to cradle her face.

"Bronwyn honey, it's Daddy."

Her eyes opened slowly, and she blinked several times. "Daddy?"

He leaned over to kiss her. "Honey, I don't want you to be scared, but you have to tell me what's been happening to you."

In spite of his attempt to soothe her, there was fear

in her eyes. "I am scared," she whispered. "I am."

"Please, honey, trust me. You don't have to be scared. I'm here, and Sam's here, and we're going to make sure that you're safe, but you have to tell me what's going on." He smiled, he hoped reassuringly. "I need to know so I can help you."

Her lower lip trembled. "I don't think you can."

The words chilled him, but even more did the look deep in those eyes. "Let me try."

She blinked again. "I'm scared I'm going to die."

"But why? A little blood from your ear and your . . . eyes? Losing a little blood doesn't mean you're going to die, sweetheart."

Bronwyn began to cry. The tears were tinged with pink. "From my eyes, Daddy?"

Wyatt hesitated; she obviously knew or suspected how extraordinary that was. "It isn't a good thing, honey, but maybe we can fix it so it doesn't happen again."

"And my ears? And my nose? And my mouth?"

He fought back a frown, not wishing to frighten her more than she already was. "You've had a nosebleed before, remember? That time in kindergarten?"

"But that was when Kenny bumped me in the nose with his head. Nobody bumped me, Daddy."

He kissed her forehead. "It's all right. It'll be all right."

Samantha had come up on the other side of the bed, and she took Bronwyn's left hand between both of hers. "Maybe Kenny's head was so hard that when he bumped you, you stayed bumped."

Bronwyn laughed.

Wyatt could have kissed Sam for that. "She's right. So I don't want you to be afraid about a little blood. I want you to tell me"—he searched her eyes—"what

272

else is scaring you."

Bronwyn took a shuddery breath, and then began.

He listened to a story about a blue light and the shivers and a voice calling, and about blood and tears and a sense of otherness—although she didn't call it that—and when she was finished, he simply nodded.

The effort of telling seemed to have exhausted her; her eyes closed and in an amazingly short time, she had fallen asleep.

Wyatt brushed the hair back from her face. "I'll take care of you, don't you worry. No one's ever going to hurt you again."

He left her in Sam's care, and started toward the West wing.

"Dr. English, what are you doing here?" Barbara Sullivan, the supervisor of nurses, had come up beside him. "I thought you left an hour ago."

He stopped, almost glad for the distraction. "I could ask the same of you," he said. Her shift was over at four and it was now nearly eight.

"I'm waiting for the police."

"Still?"

"Again."

The grim set of her mouth gave him pause. "What's happened now?"

"The cleaning crew found one of the physical therapists dead in the department."

"Dead of what?"

"Oh my. What . . ." She sighed, as if the weight of the world were upon her. "His head was crushed and his neck broken in one of the therapy machines."

Wyatt grimaced. "His, you said. It was Ernie Miller, then."

"Yes. You knew Ernie, of course."

"Of course. He gave therapy to my wife." In fact, Wyatt had noticed when he was checking Deborah's chart earlier that Miller had seen her for therapy on Friday.

"Oh yes, how foolish of me not to think of that." Barbara glanced at her watch. "Anyway, I hope they hurry. The police, I mean. I called them and had the hardest time convincing the dispatcher that there'd been another one."

"I can imagine. There've been five?"

"Yes. Five deaths in hardly any time at all."

"Do they have . . . any ideas?"

"Tons of ideas, but nothing concrete. They're looking for a connection, other than, of course, that they all worked here."

He had a strong suspicion as to what the connection was, but he kept silent, encouraging her to go on with a nod.

"Anyway, assuming the police ever do return, and if they ever manage to get poor Ernie's head pried from that machine, the sheriff has appointed a special investigator, and they're going to take all of the bodies to another facility in a 'neutral town,' as they refer to it, to conduct the autopsies."

"That's interesting."

"Hmm, very. I gather they've decided that everyone who is still alive is a suspect, including the pathologist who does our postmortems."

Wyatt had to smile at that; the pathologist, despite spending most of his time up to his elbows in bodies, was a mild-mannered man who was in line to inherit the earth. Of the hospital medical staff, he probably had the least potential as a killer.

Barbara, apparently reading his mind, smiled back. "I know, it is to laugh."

"Well, I'm sure he'll be intrigued at being a

274

suspect. He's a big mystery fan."

"He's welcome to this one," Barbara said. "Listen, I hope I'm not holding you up? You looked as though you were going somewhere, rather than roaming the halls like myself. A patient?"

"Actually, I was going over to West. . . ."

"Yes, I might have guessed that if I weren't in such a tizzy. I won't keep you then."

"Thank you, Barbara, for the information."

"Oh that." She waved a hand in dismissal. "The police will probably arrest me for releasing confidential material, but I've been here since seven this morning and I'm too tired to care. All I want is to go home."

"That's what we all want," he said.

The nurses on West looked ready to jump out of their skins even though every usable light in the place was on and blazing.

"Dr. English," one of them said, "thank heavens it's you."

Wyatt nodded his understanding; this was the shift that had normally worked with Cassie Owens. Her death, even more than the others, must have set them on edge.

"We've been sitting here driving ourselves crazy, imagining who the killer might be," the unit secretary said.

"Jason or Freddy," the first nurse said, and laughed nervously, as though she hadn't quite eliminated those possibilities.

"No," the secretary said, "it's usually the last person you'd ever suspect."

"I imagine it is," Wyatt said. "May I have my wife's chart, please?"

The secretary scooted across in her chair to retrieve the chart from the rack. "Sorry," she said, "we're all a bit schizo tonight."

"I don't wonder." He paused. "Is the dictation room open?"

"Sure. But," she called after him, "I'd lock the door after me if I were you."

The dictation room was small, wide enough to hold two narrow desks, two chairs, and a recliner which couldn't recline because of space limitations. Each desk had a Dictaphone which was hooked up to the hospital's Medical Records department.

Wyatt sat at the first desk and opened Deborah's chart.

Within a few minutes, he had the answer he'd been dreading he would find—the names of four of the five victims. He closed the chart and sat for a moment, staring off into nothingness, trying to make sense of something that defied explanation.

As a doctor, he was trained to be logical almost to a fault, and to look beneath the surface for underlying causes and effects. Those analytical skills, honed by years of practice, had—this time—brought him to a conclusion that seemed completely irrational.

The killer seemed to be . . . *Deborah*. Something Wyatt could not entirely comprehend had taken place—and somehow it had affected Bronwyn as well. An evil force had been unleashed, and at its heart lay Deborah.

There was no other answer. Was there?

Tony Armstrong, Lucille Morris, Cassie Owens, Ernie Miller.

Deborah's doctor, a lab tech, one of her nurses, her therapist.

Of the victims, only the first, the janitor, had had no direct connection to Deborah. But the man had been killed in her room, and at roughly the same time Bronwyn was having what the nurse had called a nightmare.

Tony Armstrong had been Deborah's physician of record. He had come to the hospital Saturday morning to see her. In his notes, Armstrong had written, "The patient showed no response to painful stimuli." Wyatt knew what "painful stimuli" were commonly employed.

A few minutes later, Armstrong had been set upon and killed. This, Wyatt suspected, would prove to coincide with Bronwyn's undergoing a "hysterical episode with hyperventilation response."

In the case of the laboratory tech, he himself had noticed a new bruise on Deborah's arm. A glance at the blood-test result verified that the blood had been drawn Saturday night by Lucille Morris, a short time before her death.

Bronwyn had told him that she'd had a "spell" Saturday night.

This afternoon, Cassie Owens, Deborah's nurse, had been murdered savagely while Bronwyn and Samantha were at the beach. He hadn't worked out the time estimates—was he afraid to?—but he had a sick feeling that his daughter's ordeal had occurred at approximately the same moment that the nurse was dying.

And the physical therapist? As much as he wished otherwise, he had little doubt that it had happened while Bronwyn was suffering the most recent attack in the hospital's emergency room.

Miller, he knew, had often given Deborah therapy, and the man was rumored to be tough on his patients. If he was tough on those who were able—

and apt—to complain, Wyatt could believe that he might be even rougher with those who could not.

Five deaths, all with some connection to his wife. And Bronwyn?

The voice his daughter had heard during her spells seemed to indicate some sort of telepathy.

The doctor in him considered the possibility that the mild concussion Bronwyn had sustained had served to open her mind to her mother's rage. Could it be? He didn't know; the human brain guarded its secrets well. . . .

Wyatt dropped his face into his hands—hands that were trembling. What had he done by keeping Deborah alive, by not being able to let go of her?

They'd cut the umbilical cord when Bronwyn was born, but that alone hadn't severed the union of mother and child.

He would have to do that, now.

Wyatt entered 6-West for the last time, and closed the door firmly behind him.

"Deborah?"

She didn't stir, not that she ever had, but a part of him wanted to believe if she was capable of doing what in his heart he knew she was doing, she might also be capable of fighting her way up from the coma to speak to him one last time.

"Deborah?" He approached the bed and gazed down at her. "It's Wyatt."

He'd always seen her, in his mind, the way she had been, but this time he saw the changes. He saw how thin she'd become, how her muscles had atrophied and strictured, and how prominent the bones were beneath her ashen skin.

He saw the scars on her arms from countless IVs

278

and blood draws, and bruises, both fresh and fading, from a myriad of sources.

Her hair had darkened—there was no sunshine to bring out its light—and begun to thin.

"I am so sorry," he said, and touched her face with his fingertips. "I was wrong to keep you this way. I was selfish; I know that now."

Wyatt could hear her breathing, and it seemed that her respirations were even more labored than they'd been when he'd seen her that morning.

"You wanted a baby so much," he said softly, thinking out loud. "And they took her from you. I didn't understand a lot of things, and maybe I still don't, but as much as you wanted our daughter, it must have left you . . . feeling empty. Bereft. Instead of her birth being the most joyous moment of your life, it was the taking of what was most precious to you."

Outside, the storm had resumed, and the lights flickered with each flash of lightning.

Wyatt fell silent. He lowered the bed railing and sat on the side of the bed, his eyes searching her face for any sign that somehow she was hearing him. He closed his hand around hers.

"I wish you could see her, just once. You know I named her Bronwyn Grace, as you wanted. She's so much like you, pretty and bright and funny. She has your eyes, and sometimes when she looks at me, it's almost as if . . . you were looking, too."

He brought her hand up and kissed it.

"Our daughter is everything I know you dreamed she would be, and I love her more every day. Because she's part of us, the best part. I would never let anything or anyone hurt her." He hesitated, and when he spoke again, it was in a whisper. "Not even you."

279

Thunder rattled the windows, and Wyatt felt something breaking up inside of him.

"Someone told me this morning that I couldn't save everyone. I didn't want to believe him at the time, but he was right. Maybe I shouldn't have asked them to save you, but I couldn't let you go. . . ."

The lights flickered again, and dimmed. Rain beat against the glass.

"I never told you, but they cut down our tree. I went to look one day, and it was gone. They'd put in a fountain, and I stood there staring at it, trying to remember, and . . . I couldn't."

Wyatt laid her hand beside her. He reached in his jacket pocket for the syringe he'd prepared after he'd left Bronwyn, but before coming here.

"I love you, Deborah. I have always loved you, and I always will."

He removed the blue plastic shield from the needle and held the syringe up to the light. He tapped the barrel gently to remove a tiny air bubble that he'd missed when he drew up the drug earlier.

He took a deep breath.

"I'm telling myself that this is what you want. That everything that's happened was because I'd kept you away from home too long."

He turned her arm so that the crook of her elbow was exposed. He'd forgotten to bring a tourniquet, but even without it, he found a vein quickly. The needle entered the vein and he drew back the plunger; a drop of blood was drawn in and it mixed with the morphine.

It is time, he thought, but he hesitated, averting his eyes from her for a moment to gain his composure. When he was ready, he leaned over and kissed her.

"We both love you, Deborah. But now, it's time for you to go home."

Quickly, before he could lose heart, he injected the morphine.

Then he sat beside her and waited.

It did not take long.

Again, as he had so many years ago, he carried his daughter into the house that Deborah had never lived in, but of which she'd been a part.

"Daddy?"

His arms tightened around her as he carried her up the stairs. "Yes, baby."

"Are we home?"

"We are home," he said. "We're all home."

Epilogue

December 21st

Bronwyn bounded up the stairs heading for her room, not wanting to be late.

"Young lady," Mrs. Henderson called after her, "how many times have I told you not to run up those stairs?"

"A million, I think," she said and laughed, turning and looking down at the housekeeper who was standing with her hands on her hips. "Just this once, and I won't do it anymore."

"That'll be the day."

Despite the stern look, Bronwyn knew she would have her way. "Daddy's going to be here any minute. . . ."

"Well, then, off with you."

Laughing out loud, she continued on up. She hadn't bothered to change from her ballet slippers to her regular shoes, and when she ran, it was almost like dancing.

She had laid her clothes out on the bed before she'd gone to class. She quickly stripped down to her underwear and pulled on her jeans. Her first try at putting on her T-shirt wound up backward, and she twisted it until it was on the right way.

Bronwyn moved to the dresser with the mirror and watched her reflection as she pulled the pins from her hair. The ballet teacher had begun demanding that the girls wear their hair up, pulled tightly into a bun, the way the professional ballerinas did.

She liked her hair loose. She fluffed it with her fingers.

"Bronwyn?" her father called.

"I'll be right there." Her tennis shoes were at the foot of the bed, but she was so impatient to be going, she decided not to change into them.

She grabbed a sweater from the hook behind her door, and dashed out of the room.

Her hand rested lightly on the bannister as she flew down the stairs.

Her father was by the front door and his eyes were watching her as she neared. He gestured at her slippers. "You're not changing your shoes? You can do that in the car, you know."

"I know, but I *feel* like wearing these today." She smiled at him and saw in his eyes that it was okay. "Come on, let's go."

He laughed. "All right, but no backseat driving."

The drive to the airport seemed to take forever, but Bronwyn spent the time thinking of the summer that now seemed so long ago.

After her mother's funeral, her father had taken her away on vacation to Australia. It was the first time she'd ever flown, and as she'd watched the endless miles of water pass beneath them, it almost seemed to her that she was free of the earth.

School and dance class and everything else had

been left behind, and though she was sad for a while, seeing all those new places and tasting new foods and listening to the accents of the people had drawn her out of herself.

She'd been sorry to leave, except that she knew Sam would be waiting to take care of her when they returned home.

And Sam had made the rest of the summer just as wonderful for her. They'd gone to the beach, to the park, and two or three times Sam had even managed to convince her father to close his office for an afternoon and come with them to a movie matinee.

They'd had a picnic in the attic of the house, and her father had brought down an old porch swing which at Bronwyn's request he'd sanded and painted, and put in her bedroom. Sam had bought her an armful of colored pillows, and now when she wanted to think, she lay there, swinging gently, amid the soft shades of blue and green and gray.

Sam had taken her shopping for school clothes in late July, and they'd laughed at the idea of trying on warm winter clothes in a heat wave.

Her father had promised to put in a pool.

And her dance teacher had suggested she take a special class for those girls who show more than a promise of talent.

Even school wasn't as bad as she'd feared. The kids knew that her mother had died, and they were nice to her. She didn't join any of the groups of girls, but she was friends with some.

Mrs. Henderson had returned from her sister's the week that school had started, and at first Bronwyn had been worried that things would go back to the way they'd been. But her father had "a talk" with her, and though Mrs. Henderson still had rules, and still favored a routine, there were changes in her ways as well.

Sam had flown off to London in September.

And now she was coming home for the holidays.

"Does she know, Daddy?" Bronwyn asked, tugging at her father's arm.

"I don't think so. I asked Mrs. Townsend not to say anything."

"This is gonna be great."

He smiled, his eyes on the road. "You two will be up all night talking again, I imagine."

"Oh, I don't know." She hid her own smile. "Maybe not."

At the airport, they waited for Sam's plane to land and taxi to the gate.

"Her mother really didn't tell her that we were going to meet her?"

"She promised me she wouldn't." Her father ruffled her hair. "Be still now. Watch for her . . she'll be here any minute."

And there, almost as if by magic, was Sam.

Her hair was a little longer, and she seemed a little thinner, but it was undoubtedly Sam.

"Samantha!" Bronwyn yelled, and took off running. She darted around people and dodged their luggage, and finally reached her.

"Bronwyn!" Sam swept her up in her arms.

She could feel Sam's heart pounding, as was hers. She buried her face in the soft fabric of her blouse. "I've missed you so much."

"Me too."

And then her father was there. He reached out and picked up Sam's carry-on bag.

"Doctor . . . I mean Wyatt . . . hello."

Bronwyn held her breath.

"Sam, you look fantastic."

Sam's hand went up and brushed the hair on the back of her neck. "Well, it grew back, finally. All that fog, I suppose." She held her hand out to him.

Wyatt English took Sam's hand, and gave it a little pull, so that she moved toward him. He kissed her gently on the lips.

Bronwyn grinned. It wasn't one of those kisses that made Mrs. Henderson "tsk" when she was watching TV, but as first kisses went, it would do.